"You are not bound by anything, Nikki."

He spoke softly, seductively, his French–Arabic accent rolling like warm water over her skin. "I will never force you to do anything you don't want to."

Her blush deepened. His words held promise of sex. It reminded her of the sensation of his lips against hers, and how her body had reacted against her will.

"I suspect my enemies will hire their own private investigator and do their own check into your past. But that's irrelevant to us."

Shock stabbed through her. "What! Why would they do that?"

"If you were found to be a fraud, or a criminal..."

Nikki's heart began to thud.

Was he playing her? Sensing that she really did have something to hide?

His smile deepened. "But there is nothing to worry about, right?"

"Of course not." The words almost choked in her throat.

Dear Reader,

There is something about desert tales—the burning, shifting sands; strange and mysterious cultures; powerful, dark warrior princes and kings with fierce codes of honor and a deep sense of duty—that begs us to believe, just for a moment, in fairy tale and legend.

My heroine, Nikki Hunt, gave up on fairy tales and happy endings a long time ago, after her life took a very bad turn. She's strong, fiercely independent and certainly not looking to be protected or swept off her feet by a dark and powerful prince or king. But when she inadvertently wanders into the ancient desert kingdom of Al Na'Jar with her small band of war orphans, something happens. Her reality shifts. And the desert magic begins to work.

And Nikki begins to realize, that even while grounded in harsh reality, fairy tales really can come true. Even for a woman like her.

I hope you enjoy this first tale of the SAHARA KINGS, and that the desert magic sweeps you along, just for a moment, to once upon a time in a land far away.

Loreth Anne White

LORETH ANNE WHITE

The Sheik's Command

ROMANTIC

SUSPENSE

 SILHOUETTE BOOKS

Recycling programs
for this product may
not exist in your area.

ISBN-13: 978-0-373-27679-0

THE SHEIK'S COMMAND

Visit Silhouette Books at www.eHarlequin.com

Printed in U.S.A.

Books by Loreth Anne White

Silhouette Romantic Suspense

Melting the Ice #1254
Safe Passage #1326
The Sheik Who Loved Me #1368
★The Heart of a Mercenary #1438
★A Sultan's Ransom #1442
★Seducing the Mercenary #1490
★The Heart of a Renegade #1505
†Manhunter #1537
★★Her 24-Hour Protector #1572
†Cold Case Affair #1582
††The Sheik's Command #1609

★Shadow Soldiers
★★Love In 60 Seconds
†Wild Country
††Sahara Kings

LORETH ANNE WHITE

Loreth Anne White was born and raised in southern Africa, but now lives in Whistler, a ski resort in the moody British Columbian Coast Mountain range. It's a place of vast wilderness, larger-than-life characters, epic adventure and romance—the perfect place to escape reality. It's no wonder she was inspired to abandon a sixteen-year career as a journalist to escape into a world of romantic fiction filled with dangerous men and adventurous women.

When she's not writing you will find her long-distance running, biking or skiing on the trails and generally trying to avoid the bears—albeit not very successfully. She calls this work, because it's when the best ideas come.

For a peek into her world visit her Web site, www.lorethannewhite.com. She'd love to hear from you.

To my grandfather, Johannes Schep, for showing me that magic lay between the covers of a book.

Chapter 1

The ragged tops of tall palms rustled quietly in a furnacelike breeze and the sky pressed down over the Moorish city of Na'Jar with a thick harmattan haze—fine particles of Sahara sand lifted by West African trades to choke the air with a dense, red fog.

Slowly, Nikki Hunt dismounted from her camel.

The old medina at the base of a four-lane boulevard that swept up the hill toward the palace was eerily deserted. Yet she could sense eyes watching her from dark windows cleaved into baked clay walls. A dog barked somewhere, and Nikki caught the blur of a black-garbed woman grabbing a child's hand and darting like a ghost into an alley.

Her mouth went dry.

Tensions in this ancient city were volatile after a brutal coup two months earlier had seized the life of the revered old king. And just two days ago there'd been a suicide bombing right outside the palace walls, someone trying to assassinate the new king who had yet to be officially sworn in. That's

what the Berber tribesmen in the barren Rahm Hills had told
Nikki when she'd inadvertently drifted across the border and
into the desert kingdom of Al Na'Jar. The Rahm Berbers said
it wasn't safe for a woman to travel in the country alone. Not
now. Not ever.

Nikki knew that.

North Africa was a hostile place for a female without
the protection of a man. It was why she was now dressed
as a Tuareg nomad with a heavy indigo-black turban wound
around her head, hiding all but her eyes, which were masked
by reflective sunglasses. Her bright white robe was cinched
tightly at her waist with a leather belt. A tasseled camel whip
and jambiya—an angrily curved dagger—hung from her
hip.

Under her robe she hid the .45-caliber pistol she'd taken
from the body of a rebel solider in Mauritania.

The skin on Nikki's hands and wrists had grown dark from
months under the desert sun, and with her blue-green eyes
hidden by shades, she'd so far managed to pass unharmed,
unquestioned. Any feminine gestures Nikki might not have
been able to mask were not terribly far removed from the
feminine grace inherent in some Saharan men, especially
those from the northern Mali region and parts of Algeria.

Nikki had watched them carefully, studying their economy
of movement in blistering heat. She'd mastered riding a camel.
And step by torturous step—not thinking beyond putting
one cracked and sandaled foot in front of the other—she'd
managed to shepherd her ragged band of ailing war orphans
across the arid northwestern Sahara. But after drinking stale
water from a wadi, her children had fallen ill.

And then Nikki had gotten lost, drifting so far north that
she'd unknowingly entered the small and unsettled Kingdom
of Al Na'Jar.

The Rahm Berbers had briefed Nikki about the coup and

told her about the new king. His Royal Highness Sheik Zakir Al Arif was descended from a proud and ancient line of fierce Moorish-Bedouin warriors who had ruled this kingdom for hundreds of years. They referred to their new monarch as the "Dark One" or the "Dark King" because they knew so little about him. He'd apparently been living in France before his father's assassination. The Berbers also told Nikki that after the suicide attack the new king had moved quickly to shut down his borders as he tried to determine who were his allies or enemies.

Which meant Nikki was now trapped in Al Na'Jar.

The only way out of this simmering kingdom was now through the seat of government—that walled fortress with its gleaming domes and minarets up on the hill at the end of the deserted boulevard.

If Nikki could get a decree from the Dark King granting her safe passage across Al Na'Jar to the Atlantic, she could save her orphans. From the coast she'd try to board a boat to Tenerife, one of the Canary Islands where the Mercy Missions relief organization had a base.

But her first priority was medicine—antibiotics and liquids that would balance electrolytes. Without it, some of her kids could die. Within days.

Nikki's stomach fisted with tension as she tethered her camel to an old stall in the abandoned marketplace. All around her the thick, silent stone walls were pocked from mortar fire. Cartridges still glinted gold on cobblestones—evidence of the violent battle between the Sheik's Army and the mysterious insurgents who'd mounted the coup.

Gaze flicking left to right, Nikki began to walk slowly up the ominously deserted boulevard that led to the walled castle. She held her arms out at her sides in a gesture of peace, and to show she was unarmed.

Heat quivered from the bleached tarmac and the tattered

leaves of the tall palms flanking the boulevard crackled in the hot wind.

She crested a slight rise and suddenly saw why the road was empty. A massive coil of razor wire had been hauled across the boulevard. Behind it lurked a blockade of Bradley and Abrams tanks, shimmering like a deadly mirage under the pitiless noonday heat.

Nikki swallowed.

The only safe way out of Al Na'Jar was through that military blockade, through that palace. Her kids were dying.

She *had* to do this.

She inhaled deeply, sucking down fear as she continued to move toward the tanks, arms held out wide. Mirrored sunglasses winked at her from beneath the soldiers' helmets, the dark snouts of their automatic weapons poking above the battle machinery, every muzzle trained on her. A fly buzzed around her head.

She didn't dare swat at it.

Then as Nikki took another step she crossed some invisible line and the soldiers tensed collectively. Someone screamed in Arabic for her to stay back or they would shoot.

Nikki's heart blipped, and for a second she wavered.

Think of the children. Save the children.

If she failed them now, then she would fail herself. She'd be worth nothing and might as well cease to exist entirely.

Clenching her jaw, gaze riveted on the tanks, Nikki took one more tentative step forward. And a soldier fired.

The slug pinged near her feet, showering her with tar.

She froze. "I mean no harm!" she yelled in Arabic. "I have come to see His Royal Highness, Sheik Zakir Al Arif of Al Na'Jar!"

A flurry of movement told Nikki they'd heard from her voice that she was female. And foreign.

All turned deadly silent.

Heat pressed down.

Nikki moistened her cracked lips as she tried to summon the mental calm she'd depended on while performing operations, back in her other life when she was still a surgeon. "I am a nurse!" she called out. "I come only in peace! I need humanitarian aid and safe passage for a group of sick children."

Silence hung heavy, broken only by desert wind rustling through palm fronds.

Carefully telegraphing her movements, Nikki reached up, removed her sunglasses, dropping them with a clatter to the hot road. Next she unwound her dark turban, letting it fall to her feet. Long hair tumbled down about her shoulders, gleaming like spun gold under the hazy red sun. She held her arms out again, shaking inside. "I am an American!" Her voice cracked. She cleared her throat. "I work with Mercy Missions, a UNICEF organization. I come in peace!"

There was another ripple of movement among the troops, and a lone soldier edged his helmeted head above a tank. He barked an order in crisp Arabic, instructing Nikki to set her dagger on the road. She unsheathed her jambiya, crouched down and placed it at her feet.

The soldier then ordered her to place proof of identity alongside the dagger and once she had done so to walk backward a hundred yards, then wait. If she moved, they would kill her.

Nikki removed her passport and nursing papers from a pouch beneath her belt. She placed the documents on the road next to her dagger, then walked slowly backward, arms out wide. Heat burned on her uncovered head as she squinted into the burning orange haze.

A portion of razor wire was drawn back from the boulevard and three soldiers approached, automatic weapons trained on her.

A pearl of sweat trickled down her belly under her robe as she waited.

One of the soldiers retrieved her documents, quickly flipped through them. He glanced up at her, then nodded curtly.

The second soldier frisked Nikki, found her pistol, disarmed her and removed the clip. Her turban was then shoved back into her hands, and with angry gestures she was ordered to recover her head.

Hands shaking, Nikki fumbled to drape the indigo cloth over her hair like a veil, flipping the fabric over her mouth and nose, leaving only her now-naked eyes exposed.

With the business end of a rifle pressed into the small of her back she was marched toward the blockade.

It was much cooler inside the palace, under the soaring mosaic arches and high domes of stained glass. But after weeks out in the desert—she'd lost count of how many—Nikki felt trapped, edgy.

The guards ushered her along a labyrinth of marbled passageways and into a large chamber. The double doors thudded brusquely behind her. She heard a bolt being driven home across the outside.

Prisoner.

Claustrophobia tightened her chest. Slowly she turned, taking in her surroundings. Marbled keyhole arches opened onto a high-walled garden lush with citrus trees and flowers. Stone fountains carved in the shapes of lions' heads tinkled water into pools and birds darted between sweet-scented orange blossoms. Nikki hadn't seen songbirds in a long time and the sound of water forced her to swallow reflexively, a potent reminder of the thirst she'd been desperately trying to ignore.

The design of the palace was similar to the Moorish architecture she'd seen in Marrakech and Casablanca.

Morocco bordered Al Na'Jar to the north, and Nikki had visited the country on her honeymoon—before she'd had the twins.

When her name used to be Alexis Etherington.

Cold nausea slicked into her stomach. She shuddered, blocking the memories of her loss, her past, forcing herself to stay present and focused. Her gaze settled on a bowl of purple grapes alongside a crystal pitcher of water and ice.

Nikki turned abruptly away from it. She could not eat and drink while her orphans still suffered. Time stretched interminably and she grew hotter under her veil, the fabric ratcheting up her cloying sense of claustrophobia and whispering panic.

Then suddenly, she heard the clip of boot heels on the smooth tiles outside the barred double doors. And something else, a sharp clicking. She tensed, spun to face the door, blood thudding in her ears, hands fisting nervously at her sides.

An order was barked outside in rough Arabic, and she heard the men announce the king.

The massive bolt slammed back, and the doors were swung wide-open with a crash. In their place stood the dark, Moorish-Bedouin warrior monarch the Berber tribesmen had told her about.

Nikki caught her breath.

The king stepped into the room, his electric presence seeming to flow out ahead of him, filling space like something that abhorred a vacuum. And Nikki realized what the other sound was that she'd heard outside the door—dogs. Because as the "Dark King" moved, three tall and slender salukis flowed like mercury at his side.

His Royal Highness Sheik Zakir Al Arif fixed glittering obsidian eyes on her, his burning attention absorbing her completely. He remained silent for a beat, then with a curt flick of his wrist he motioned for his guards to step outside.

Nikki noticed the king's personal guards were not dressed like the other soldiers of the Sheik's Army. They wore bloodred turbans that covered most of their faces, bright white tunics, and they had unusual long knives sheathed at their hips. The men retreated in unison with a silent bow of their heads, the massive doors swinging shut behind them.

Nikki pressed her damp hands firmly against her robes in an effort to stop the sudden shaking. She had no idea of royal protocol, no knowledge of the rules or traditions of this land. She spoke only a smattering of Arabic. But she could speak French, and with Al Na'Jar once having been a protectorate of France, there was a good chance French was still spoken here as a language of business and diplomacy.

Nikki wasn't sure what she had expected of the mysterious monarch, either, but it sure as hell wasn't this. He was tall—well over six feet, all lean muscle. And his looks were the dark smoldering stuff of feminine desert fantasy—high-bridged aquiline nose; glittering, hooded obsidian eyes; sensual yet predatory features; rich skin; blue-black hair; heavy brows; aggressive jaw; and beautiful, beautiful lips. And his exotic physique was reinforced by his dress—a brocade Arabic tunic over riding pants, tall leather boots, a bejeweled scimitar sheathed at his hips. The effect was mesmerizing.

Disconcerting.

But more than anything it was the utter physical confidence with which he moved and the naked directness of his gaze that felt most intimidating. Because in addition to radiating power, Sheik Zakir Al Arif radiated sexual charisma. He was undeniably physically attractive—if you liked them tall, dark and decidedly dangerous. And once upon a time, when Nikki had thought about men in her life, that was the way she liked them.

She inhaled quietly, suddenly grateful for the protection of her veil, waiting for him to make the first move.

"American?" he said, taking a step closer.

She nodded, half bowing, half curtsying.

His black eyes lasered directly into hers. "Your documents identify you as Nicola Ann Hunt."

He spoke perfect English in a French accent laced with the guttural and oh-so-sensual undertones of Arabic. The tone of his voice dipped between baritone and bass. Mellifluous. And it seemed to ripple like water over her skin.

"Just Nikki," she offered, her voice catching. "Nikki Hunt."

His brow lowered, and Nikki had to force herself not to retreat a step.

"From Washington, D.C.?"

"No," she lied, a gut reaction. "I mean, yes, I…was born there." Any remnant of confidence Nikki might have retained during her ordeal at the blockade had just been ripped from as her the king vocalized an element of her past.

"Do you realize how close you came to being killed!" he barked suddenly, eyes flashing, neck muscles tense.

She flinched, remaining silent.

"Just two days ago," he snapped, "an insurgent dressed in women's robes blew himself up right outside the palace gates. Killed five of my men. My troops now have orders to shoot— and kill—anyone who dares approach the blockade against orders. Female or not." He stepped closer, lowering his voice to a smooth guttural growl. "The only reason you are alive, Ms. Hunt—" he glowered down at her "—is because my men *disobeyed* those orders. For that they will be punished. But what I want to know is, what are you doing here? And what do you want from me?" It was a command, not a question.

Nikki had to force herself to meet his aggressive black eyes. "I…I'm a nurse with Mercy Missions," she said, breath hot against her veil. "It's a global relief organization affiliated to UNICEF and the Red Cross—"

"You're a missionary?"

"No, just a nurse with a mission-based organization."

"What is your religious affiliation?"

A spurt of defiance shot through her, and she welcomed it. "That's not your business."

His left brow hooked up, a sign of vague amusement. He took another step closer, his dogs moving in concert at his heels, and Nikki's sense of entrapment tightened like a noose. Along with it came another edgy rush of adrenaline. Fight or flight, she told herself. That's what she was experiencing. And flight was not exactly a choice right now.

"Understand one thing, Ms. Hunt," he said, his voice going quiet, gravelly. "*Everything* in Al Na'Jar is my business."

"I don't have any religious affiliation," she answered softly.

Any faith I ever had deserted me that Christmas Eve on an icy road.

"Then you will not object to being asked to remove your veil so I can see who I am dealing with?" Another order.

She reached up, slowly unwrapped the fabric covering her head and face. Her hair tumbled in soft waves around her shoulders.

Shock rippled visibly through the king—his first sign of unguarded emotion.

He stared into her face, then brazenly, hotly, swept his glance over her entire body. The sensation was intimate, electric. Silence hung for several beats, broken only by the gentle sound of water trickling into a pool outside. "Why," he said finally, very quietly, "did you risk your life to come and see me, Ms. Hunt?"

"I need your help," she said.

One side of his mouth curved up slightly. "And what makes you think I will help you?"

She moistened her dry lips, and his gaze dipped disconcertingly to her mouth as she searched for the right words.

"Because if you don't, my children will die."

Chapter 2

Zakir's heart beat cool and steady as his gaze cut into hers. His mistrust of this woman was deep and it was instant. But so was his interest—on too many levels.

She was the most striking thing he'd ever seen. He'd been rocked when she'd removed her veil to reveal a tangle of strawberry-blond curls, fine-boned features, sunburned cheeks. Her wide turquoise eyes—the first thing about her that had rattled Zakir on sight—were reminiscent of deep, cool oasis pools.

A man could drown in eyes like that was his initial off-the-wall thought.

His second thought was that those eyes looked haunted, empty. And the way her gaze held his was so direct and provocative that she appeared to have been stripped of normal social veils and wiles. It was as if this woman had absolutely nothing to lose.

And it threw him for a minute.

Maybe he was just shaken by how close his men had come to killing her. On his orders. On his soil.

He knew what that could mean—an innocent and photogenic U.S. aid worker shot dead on his doorstep would grip international headlines and quite possibly destroy the tentative dialogue Zakir was trying to cultivate with the United States as he tried to reopen Al Na'Jar to foreign diplomatic missions.

Or perhaps he was rattled because this lone woman had actually managed to enter his country, defy the Sheik's Army blockade and was now inside the very heart of his palace. She could quite possibly be the enemy sent to harm him. One thing Zakir had learned over these past two traumatic months was that no one in Al Na'Jar could be trusted, and nothing was quite what it seemed.

His enemies were bold. They were faceless. They appeared to be old-school traditionalists intent on destroying the Al Arif Moorish-Bedouin dynasty. And Zakir was convinced they had operatives—traitors—right inside these very palace walls, sitting right on his own King's Council.

Zakir didn't yet know who was orchestrating or funding this move to wipe out the bloodline that had ruled this desert nation for hundreds of years, but he was certain it had been sparked by the discovery of large oil reserves and his father's subsequent attempts to move the ancient kingdom into line with the new world.

Whatever the motive, he needed time to flush the Brutus out from his own council. And he needed the United States as an ally now more than ever. He had to tread carefully with this woman, whoever she was.

Snapping his fingers, he motioned for his dogs to go lie quietly under the arches that led to the small garden, but his eyes didn't leave Nikki's for an instant.

He took a step closer to her, and she straightened her spine, jaw tilting up. This was clearly a woman who stood her ground.

It intrigued Zakir further. He studied her carefully, taking in every detail of her features, every nuance of her energy.

He noted that the backs of her hands were deeply sun browned, her right hand calloused at the junction of the thumb and index finger, where a lead rope of a belligerent camel might rub one raw. Her leather sandals were old, broken, her feet dirty. Her cheeks were burned and freckled. She looked thin. Tired. Dusty. As if she'd been traveling for some time through the sands of the Sahara.

He held out his hand suddenly, palm up in a magnanimous gesture toward the table. "Please sit down, take some water, some fruit," he said.

Her eyes flickered toward the table, but she remained standing. "Thank you, but I didn't come for water. I came for your help."

So she wasn't going to accept his hospitality, in spite of herself. This was an insult to Al Na'Jar culture and thus to him. Curiosity, interest rustled deeper into Zakir, in spite of himself.

"What kind of help? What children are you talking about?"

"I need medicines. And I need your permission to escort seven war orphans through Al Na'Jar to the Atlantic coast where I need to take a ship to the Canary Islands. I also need to contact the Mercy Missions headquarters on the island of Tenerife."

He crooked up his brow. "Seven orphans?"

"We were nine," she said quietly. "I lost two. And I can't say for certain that they are all orphans, but it will take time to find out if any of their parents are alive. If that can even be done at this stage."

"Where are these children now?"

"I left them in the care of Berber tribesmen in the Rahm Hills."

Disbelief instantly snaked through Zakir. Rahm Berbers were notoriously—and violently—hostile toward outsiders. They took no prisoners, asked no questions—simply sliced the throats of interlopers and left their bodies in the desert.

"And where do these orphans come from?"

"From the mission outpost at which I was working in Mauritania."

He angled his jaw, suspicion growing in him. "There is civil unrest in Mauritania. The north is now a rebel-held region."

She looked suddenly drained. "Yes," she said quietly. "I fled with the children when the rebels came to burn the mission." Her wide eyes glimmered for a moment, but some deep ferocity inside her flattened any emotion and her features tightened once again. "The rebels came with machetes. They killed the nuns, the priest, the doctor and two aid workers from Belgium—hacked them to pieces. And they murdered most of the children. I fled with those I could."

Zakir studied her long and hard. "How did you get all the way from Mauritania to Al Na'Jar?"

"Over the Sahara."

"You crossed the western Sahara from Mauritania?"

"On foot, with two camels."

"Dressed like this, like a Tuareg nomad?"

"One of my children is fourteen years old, and…" Her voice hitched and Zakir could see her struggling again, digging down deep for control and losing, because her eyes once again brimmed with moisture. "The fourteen-year-old posed as my wife. We traveled with the younger children as a family unit."

As captivated as Zakir was by her story, he couldn't buy it.

Sure, people crossed the desert on foot. Bedouin families routinely traversed the Sahara. So did the odd German tourist group in big powered trucks. Or the occasional thrill-seeking American on camel. And yes, political refugees were known to have fled places from as far as southern Nigeria, sometimes taking nine months to a year to cross the Sahara on foot into Morocco, making it up to Spanish Ceuta only to be imprisoned in holding pens as they dreamed of passage across the Mediterranean to Europe.

But this woman, alone? With a band of ailing young orphans?

The Sahara was a wild, lawless place. An ocean of shifting, burning sand. Disorientating. The endless space, thirst and heat played tricks with one's mind. There were none of the usual touchstones most Western women would be accustomed to.

"How did you know which way to travel?" he said, watching her face for signs of a lie.

"A camel dealer in a small village told me which stars to follow and where the moon and sun should be in the sky in relation to myself if I wanted to walk northwest."

"That's…a suicide mission."

"And our only option. Otherwise we'd be dead at the hands of rebels. We had to take the risk."

"How long did this journey take?"

She cast her eyes down and he followed her gaze, saw where her skin had been abraded by sand under the old leather of her sandals, and again he noted the chafing on her hand.

"Two months, maybe less…or more," she said softly. "I… it's confusing. I lost track."

Zakir felt an involuntary squeeze of compassion in his chest. He warned himself this was dangerous, because her story was wild. She could be a consummate actress milking his empathy, blinding him to the real reason she was here. She could have been sent by someone who knew his weakness for striking women and sex. He was notorious in the West for his constant string of high-profile female conquests. And the more challenging the conquest, the more satisfying the consummation. The thrill of seduction and the triumph of sex was Zakir's drug of choice. His stress release. Something that made the alpha adrenaline junkie in him *feel*.

And he'd always gotten what he wanted.

But things were different now.

Now he had a duty. To his people, to his country. To his father's memory and to the Al Arif bloodline. Now he could not afford to make mistakes or people would die.

"Al Na'Jar is not exactly en route from Mauritania to the Canary Islands," he said brusquely, irritation surfacing at the notion he could potentially be manipulated by his own libido. At the cost of his throne and nation—and his own life.

Tension stiffened her body. She narrowed her turquoise eyes. "Entering Al Na'Jar was a mistake. I was aiming for the coastline of Western Sahara—"

"The Western Sahara is a lawless country ruled by guerilla activists and tribesmen—"

"It's also the closest route to the sea," she interrupted. "Like you said, Al Na'Jar isn't exactly en route."

"So you just happened to stray miles farther north, into my kingdom?"

Her cheeks heated and her eyes glittered with mounting indignation. "I told you—I lost direction. I crossed into Al Na'Jar at the Rahm foothills by mistake. I had zero intention of coming this far north, or getting stuck here."

"And hostile Berber tribesmen just happened to take in your children and point the way to my palace?"

"Look, I don't know who you think I am, but if you give me what I need, I'll be out of your castle and out of your hair before nightfall."

His heart beat faster at the spurt of aggression burning into her features. But he still didn't trust this story.

"You are lucky." He took a step closer, purposefully

invading her personal space, testing her boundaries. "Because those Rahm Berbers ordinarily kill a mysterious Tuareg in their territory on sight. Yet they did not." He lowered his voice. "Why?"

She held his gaze, her cheeks flushing deeper with angry frustration. And Zakir's blood zinged. This woman had a raw, primal intensity. She was stripped of all pretense, down to the very basics. And his skin tingled with unwanted sexual energy as he felt himself heat.

"I've never been lucky," she countered crisply.

"Oh, yes, you most definitely are, Ms. Hunt. You are still alive. And now you have wandered into my country, and my palace—a much safer place for you than Western Sahara."

"Is it really safer?" she whispered.

Heat arrowed through Zakir's belly. Deep inside he wondered if she'd be this bold and direct in bed. Yet he sensed that beyond her fiery wall lay a vulnerable and tender part, and if he managed to break through she'd become sweet and soft in his arms. Zakir felt an anticipatory sensual rush at this thought, and the hint of a smile briefly toyed along his lips.

She noticed it, and defiance crackled afresh in those oasis eyes. "So, are you able to help me? Your highness," she added with barely disguised disdain.

He regarded her in intense silence for several beats, then shook his head.

"You play me for a fool, Ms. Hunt," he said coolly. He swiveled on his boot heels and strode toward the doors, hand on the jeweled hilt of his scimitar.

"Wait, please!"

He stopped, turned slowly to face her.

Her fists balled at her sides. "You're saying you *won't* help me?"

"I'm saying I don't believe you. You will remain in my

palace for the night, under my guard." He banged on the door with the base of his fist and barked an order in Arabic.

"My men will escort you to guest chambers. Meanwhile, I shall have your story and credentials verified with—"

Horror swamped her features and she lurched forward. "I can't stay here! I *must* get back to my children. They need that medicine *now.*"

He held up his hand, warning her back as his guards entered the chamber. "Your passport and story must be checked. Meanwhile, make a list of the supplies you need. We will discuss it when I summon you to my dining hall tonight."

She clasped his arm, desperation now glimmering nakedly in her eyes, and Zakir's chest tightened, along with his groin. A most inappropriate reaction, but this woman—her touch—did something to him. He flattened his mouth, tamping down any emotion, and he glowered down at her hand on his arm.

"Your highness, I beg of you," she whispered. "My children are with tribal mountain people. I don't know how long they will remain safe. One—the fourteen-year-old girl I told you about—is pregnant and is experiencing complications. She needs me."

Zakir motioned to his guards to remove her. They took hold of her arms, pulling her toward the door.

"Please!" Tears of frustration that she could no longer hold back tracked through the dust on her cheeks as she struggled to resist his guards. "You don't understand! The child was raped by a rebel soldier. She's carrying the rebel's baby—"

"Take her away, now!" he barked, furious, not wanting to watch the pain on this woman's face any longer. Not wanting to show the slightest weakness in front of his men.

"You bastard!" she yelled at him, fighting against his guards as they dragged her from the chamber. "You have no right to hold me prisoner!"

He heard her swearing at his men as the doors thudded shut.

The room went silent.

Zakir exhaled slowly.

Clasping his hands behind his back, he walked over to the arches that opened onto his garden. His trio of salukis surged silently to his side.

He inhaled the scent of gardenia and orange blossom as he watched small birds dart around the fountain. It reminded him of his holiday estate in southern Spain, where he'd rather be. He'd never expected—or desired—to rule this kingdom. It had happened so suddenly, under such tragic circumstances.

But this was his duty now. To Al Na'Jar. To his people. To his heritage.

And holding Nikki Hunt overnight in order to verify her story was the prudent thing.

One wrong move could bring down this entire fragile kingdom and bring great harm to his people.

Besides, he could not in good conscience allow a foreign woman out there alone. It was not safe. Especially now that dusk approached. This was for her own good.

And his.

Because if the nurse really was who she claimed to be, she could still be captured by his enemy and used as leverage against him.

Either way, Nikki Hunt was potentially as dangerous to him as she was beautiful.

Perhaps it was already too late. Because already Zakir felt the siren call of a new sexual conquest. Already a small and dangerous coal of physical lust for that woman was simmering deep in his gut. And the fact she could be an enemy just deepened the forbidden element, added a sensual intensity.

These longings were things that Zakir had not intended feeling once he took the throne. And it was certainly not something Zakir could act upon. Not now.

Not ever.

For his life had changed—because of a traitor who lurked within these very castle walls.

Chapter 3

Nikki stalked through the massive guest chambers, flung open the gilt French doors and stepped onto a small balcony. A blast of desert heat slammed into her and her heart sank as she took in the dense, orange fog obscuring distant minarets. Dusk was also crawling in over the ancient Moorish city, and with it came a suffocating sense of oppression.

She peered over the balustrade. Far below lay a square of fragrant garden enclosed by high walls topped with ornate turrets. She'd have to be a ninja to scale those, if she could even find a way down there. Nikki swore softly to herself.

She'd come so very far on a journey of epic proportions. She'd shepherded those poor kids for months over the desert, protecting them, feeding them, caring for them. She had become their mother, their father, their friend and guardian. And she'd been forced to endure the pain of burying two already. Saving those orphans had become Nikki's sole reason for being.

Yet now she was being thwarted, held captive in some egotistical sheik's castle? No way in hell.

She had to get out. But how?

His words growled through her mind. *Meanwhile, I shall have your story and credentials verified...*

Nikki shut her eyes, gripping her fingers tightly around the balustrade as a sudden wave of nausea engulfed her, panic clouding her brain like a stifling hood.

Would her identity hold?

It had taken her seven long, tortuous years and a trip halfway around the world to finally lose herself in the North African desert, to find a measure of freedom from the ghosts that haunted her. The last thing on this earth she needed now was for some arrogant sheik to steal that away from her by digging into her past.

If Zakir's probing alerted her husband to the fact she was alive, Senator Sam Etherington would stop at *nothing* to drag her back to the States. He'd see that she was arrested for assuming a false identity, traveling on a forged passport, working with fraudulent nursing papers, not appearing in court to face the massive civil suit he'd smacked her with. Sam would do it all—and more—just to punish her for having gotten away.

And for having their children in her car on the night he'd tried to have her run off the road.

She began to shake at the thought, the memories. And the taste of hatred—and fear—filled her mouth.

The newspaper coverage, the public torment, the humiliation, her downward spiral into alcohol and drugs...it would all start again. And this time she wasn't sure she could survive.

Nikki didn't care about the dying part. The person she once was had "died" already. But those orphans were her sole purpose, her reason to keep fighting. Where she hadn't been able to save her own toddler twins, she *could* still save these kids.

If Zakir would agree to help them.

Spinning around, Nikki stormed back into the room. She grabbed a jug from a dark wood table, sloshed water into a glass and drank deeply. Blocks of ice bumped against her lip, and she could taste mint. But as she thought of her children the cool water turned bitter, and she set the glass down sharply. How could she in good conscience quench her thirst, bathe and dress herself in the ridiculously lavish robes provided for her in the cupboards of this room when her orphans were out there suffering?

She marched to the door, began thumping it with the base of her fist.

A guard swung the door open, abruptly bringing Nikki face to blade with a long gleaming knife. Breath snared in her throat. She raised both hands, backing off slowly. "It's okay," she whispered. "I'm sorry. No harm."

The guard shut the door, locked it.

She ran her trembling hands over her dust-thickened hair. Fine. She'd do it the king's way. She'd bathe, dress in the idiotic finery that had been laid out for her, write out her list of supplies and then she'd wait for his royal damn highness to summon her to his great hall for dinner.

She'd play by his rules—it was her only choice.

Zakir caught his breath as his guards ushered Nikki into the dining hall, but outwardly he controlled himself, motioning silently for his dogs to remain seated where he stood in front of a massive portrait done in dark, sweeping oils.

He was learning to communicate with his hounds using only hand signals. The dogs themselves had been trained by a female K-9 operative from a private military organization based off the west coast of Africa. Zakir's brother Omair had quietly arranged this because no one could know why Zakir needed the dogs. The traitor on his own King's Council would potentially use this knowledge to challenge Zakir's right to the throne and destroy him.

Until Zakir had taken the official oath and been officially sworn in as King of Al Na'Jar, he could display absolutely no sign of weakness. Besides, traditional Arabic hunting dogs were a fitting accompaniment for a desert monarch. Salukis were said to be the earliest breed of domestic dog to have diverged from wolves, and historically they had traveled with nomadic tribes over an area stretching from the Sahara Desert across the Middle East all the way to the Caspian Sea. Ghorab, Khaya and Tala would not pique unwanted curiosity.

And once Zakir was fully sworn in, he could move quickly to unilaterally change the constitution and protect his power. And thus the country.

Under a new constitution, his dark secret would no longer matter.

The only reason Zakir had not already taken the oath was because the current constitution stated that before a new king could be officially crowned, he had to have a queen. The archaic laws had been written this way as a means of ensuring heirs. This would all change once his power was officially enshrined.

Finding a wife, however, was the very least of Zakir's problems right now. His priority was to stabilize the volatile political situation and root out the traitors before he met the same end as his father, mother and older brother.

And once he learned who the traitors were, and who had assassinated his parents and older brother, Zakir would need to show boldness—ruthlessness—in his punishment.

Nothing less than a public beheading of the criminals would be expected.

These would be the first and last public executions of

Zakir's reign. He had no stomach for this ancient form of justice. It was yet another law he would abolish once he seized full control of his council and country.

But he *would* need a wife, soon. An emissary in Paris had already started a low-profile search for a candidate. Once the list of potential women had been narrowed, Zakir would interview them himself. His top choice would be offered a carefully drafted contract to serve as queen.

He did not think this would be a problem. He'd never had a shortage of stunning females willing to appear on the arm of a dashing tycoon sheik. And at this stage of his life he did not have the luxury of thinking he might marry for love. Zakir had only ever truly loved once. He doubted it would happen again. That one experience—and the ensuing betrayal—had almost cost him and his family everything.

But as Nikki walked slowly up to him, a vision in a white robe, Zakir felt a small pang of regret. Along with it came a whisper of yearning, a sense of aloneness.

He shook it off. This was how it must be now.

Yet his thoughts drifted again as the hundreds of candles in the room transformed Nikki's hair into a halo of spun gold.

Zakir hated the candles. They threw too many quivering shadows, blurred colors, and made halos in his vision as they were doing with her hair now. But dinner by candlelight was a palace tradition Zakir would have to change slowly. Again, he wanted no reason to alert anyone to his weakness. He needed to telegraph absolute strength.

His heart beat faster as Nikki approached and Zakir found himself straightening his spine. As she came closer, he saw that her robe was shot through with bold threads of gold. She'd piled her freshly washed hair up on her head in a careless fashion, loose tendrils escaping a clasp to fall softly about her face.

Her allure, Zakir realized—angling his head slightly to the

side so he could use his peripheral vision to see her better—was in the way she managed to come across as radiantly natural yet sensually elegant at the same time. A mesmerizing cocktail that made him want to know her deeper, to find out who she really was inside.

Up close he saw that she wore no makeup even though Zakir's guest quarters provided for everything a woman might want. He could detect no fragrance, either, apart from a soft hint of coconut oil that she'd obviously used to soften her desert-dry skin after she'd bathed. A little spurt of heat quivered inside Zakir as she came almost within touching distance. He had to tamp down a sudden urge to reach out for her.

She stopped directly in front of him, her turquoise eyes tunneling pointedly into his. Zakir felt himself falling, drowning into the intensity of her gaze. She thrust a piece of paper at him. "Here is my list of supplies." There was no smile, no warmth in her voice.

Zakir took the note from her, a frisson of electricity arcing up his arm and crackling into his chest as his skin connected with hers. He swallowed, shocked, and set the note on a table beneath a massive oil portrait of his father. "You'll have what you need by daybreak if your papers check out."

"You're not going to read it?"

He couldn't, not in this light.

"My assistant will take care of everything." He held his hand out, diverting her attention toward the table. "Please, do take a seat. My chefs will be bringing in the main course shortly. In the meantime, some wine."

Instead of complying, Nikki's attention shifted to the bold oil study of Zakir's father on the wall behind him. She stepped closer to it, peering up at the burning, coal-black eyes, dark brows, aristocratic nose and sharp cheekbones of His Highness Sheik Ahmed Al Arif.

"Is that him? The previous king?"

"My father, yes."

"You have his features," she said quietly, absorbed by the painting. She turned suddenly and looked directly into his eyes. Zakir's stomach tensed. There was something so visceral and intelligent about this woman that she made his blood tingle. But she was making him edgy, too, as if she could see right into his secret vulnerability. He didn't like this. Very little in life made Zakir truly nervous. He reached down to touch the head of Ghorab, drawing reassurance from the dog. Her gaze followed his hand, and again Zakir felt she could detect something.

She turned and began to walk slowly along the wall, studying each of the oils that lined the length of the great dining hall as she went. The paintings depicted his family tree, ranging back to antique portraits of legendary Al Arif warrior sheiks posed on prized stallions with hooded falcons on their arms, all the way to an image of Zakir and his family that had been painted when he was younger.

Zakir watched Nikki move, the slight sway of her hips. She carried herself with unconscious ease. Yet he could sense her calculating, scheming.

Nikki paused in front of the large family painting with Zakir in it. "Are those your siblings?" she said, gazing up at the massive work of art.

He came up behind her, closer than was necessary, and her body braced in his proximity. But she didn't move away. It fed something deep and primal inside Zakir, and he inhaled her scent, felt her warmth. "That's my younger sister, Dalilah." Zakir pointed over Nikki's shoulder, bringing himself closer yet, almost touching her. "And those are my two younger brothers, Tariq and Omair. Standing behind them is my older brother, Da'ud." Zakir hesitated, feeling a sharp stab of grief. "Da'ud was killed two months ago," he said softly.

She turned to face him and their eyes met. Electricity zinged, palpable, as if there was a crackling force around her. "Killed? How?"

"Assassinated in his bed on his private yacht off Barcelona. A band of men came in the night, sliced his throat down with a ceremonial Al Na'Jar jambiya."

"How do you know it was a local ceremonial knife?"

He crooked his brow up. "It was the opinion of the coroner that the murder weapon was a ceremonial dagger. It has a very specific curve. This opinion was confirmed by a private medical practitioner, of course."

"You mean his killers were making some kind of political statement?"

"By using that knife? Yes, along with the fact that Da'ud was slain on the very same night that my father and my mother were killed right here in this palace, as they slept." Zakir watched carefully for her reaction. He wanted to get a read on her. If she *was* involved with his enemies, she might betray herself.

She stared at him, scrutinizing in return. "So that's how you became king? Someone wanted *you* to lead, as opposed to Da'ud?"

"My enemies don't want me as king, Nikki. They tried to kill me, too."

"You mean…the suicide bomb the other day?"

"No. Even before the bomb there was a break-in at my home in Paris, on the very same night that Da'ud and my parents were assassinated. A ceremonial dagger was left on my pillow. I suspect that if I'd been home that night, I'd be dead, too."

"But you weren't home?"

"I was…in the bed of a female companion." He smiled bleakly. "It appears that in this case sleeping around was good for my health."

Nikki felt her cheeks flush as she tamped down a sudden

mental picture of Zakir naked in bed. But it was too late—the image was lodged firm, and she felt her blood heat.

She could see in Zakir's face that he knew it, too. He was toying with her sexually, finding her reaction amusing. But the glint in his eyes faded slowly along with his smile. "I never expected to lead this country, Nikki."

And in those words Nikki sensed real reluctance, sorrow even. Empathy touched her. Compassion was not an emotion she could fight. Nikki lived to heal. It was part of her nature, part of what had steered her into medicine.

"What were you doing before this?" she asked quietly. "Apart from sleeping around, I mean."

His lips curved again, slowly. "You have a sense of humor."

"What I have, your highness, is a really desperate need to get out of here."

There was no smile this time. He walked over to an ornate credenza, touched a bottle of wine lightly with his fingertips and tilted his head in question. "White wine or red? Or something stronger, perhaps?"

"I don't drink." She said it too quickly, and she felt her cheeks heat.

A frown twitched over his brow as he poured himself a glass of red. "It's a pity. This is a fine merlot from my estate in the south of Spain. Can I perhaps get you something else?"

"You could get me my passport, medicines and safe passage to Tenerife," she said, swiftly changing the subject.

He snorted softly, swirling his glass. "In time, Nikki. If your papers and story check out, you will be free to go by morning." He sipped his wine, watching her over the rim.

"My children don't have the luxury of time, Zakir."

"Nor does my country. And that is where my duty lies." He came up to her, the bulb of his wineglass resting easily in the crook of his fingers, and she noted his hands were beautiful—long, strong, tapered fingers. Dusky skin. She swallowed, again trying to erase the disturbing image of Zakir's naked body against crisp white sheets.

"I might have lived in Europe, Nikki, but I was raised here in Al Na'Jar." He turned his gaze toward his family portrait. "From a young age I was taught by my father to accept that this land, this desert, was my heritage and that it would be my foremost duty if I was ever called upon. So even though I was only second in the line of succession I was still taught the skills required of a desert monarch—the arts of horsemanship, falconry, hunting Arabic-style with salukis. I learned the dialects of the region and I studied the local cultures, the conflicts between Sahara tribes. My father made sure I also knew how to live as a nomad in the desert, and I did my time in military training. But after the military, while Da'ud remained here in Al Na'Jar to be groomed for the throne, I was sent overseas to study economics at the Sorbonne in Paris. After which I took the helm of the Al Arif Corporation, which deals primarily in commodities—oil, uranium, diamonds, along with a very extensive network of global real estate holdings, including summer and winter resorts around the world."

He sipped his wine slowly, and Nikki's gaze was lured to his lips. "Those were my riches, Nikki," he said quietly. "The economy was my kingdom. I was not a desert raider as my ancestors were, but rather a corporate warrior. And now I find myself here, in a land trapped somewhere back in the middle ages. My duty is now to follow my father's lead and build a bridge to the twenty-first century." He inhaled deeply. "But as you have seen I have enemies. And I believe those enemies will not stop until they have wiped out the entire Al Arif bloodline. They are bold, and they are highly creative. And then you show up—a mysterious lone woman just appearing at my palace. *This* is the reason you must remain under my guard until I can verify your story."

Nikki moistened her lips, disturbed by the heat pooling low in her belly as Zakir's smoldering eyes pierced hers, as his rich accent rippled warm over her skin. "For all I know, Zakir," she said, her voice going husky, "you are behind the coup yourself, because *you* wanted the throne. It would be conceivable, for example, for you to have staged the so-called attempt on your life in Paris in order to look innocent."

Surprise glimmered momentarily in his features. Then his eyes narrowed sharply and Nikki felt a cool whisper of fear rising in her. She'd overstepped her bounds. But he smiled suddenly, a bright slash of white against dark skin, and his black eyes glittered. Fear rippled deeper, his aggressive smile sparking something disturbingly primal in Nikki. He really was arrogant—and too damn beautiful for his own good. She quickly returned her attention to the family portrait in an effort to hide the unwelcome sexual interest she had no doubt was showing in her own eyes.

But as she studied the massive family painting, a disturbing familiarity in the features of his brother Tariq began to niggle at her. "If someone truly wanted to wipe out the entire Al Arif bloodline—" she frowned up at Tariq's image, trying to place where she might possibly have seen his distinctive, aggressive features "—then why were your younger brothers not attacked as well, or your sister?"

"Tariq is in the United States—"

The niggle of cold discomfort burrowed deeper into Nikki. Somehow she knew that.

"Dalilah is also in America," said Zakir. "Perhaps my enemies had a problem coordinating an attempt on their lives halfway around the world, in a country that aggressively watches its borders. Or possibly we thwarted them before they could act, because mere hours after the assassinations we retained the services of a top global security company to protect both Dalilah and Tariq. I also brought some of the company's close protection personnel here with me to Al Na'Jar—bodyguards initially trained as Gurkha militia in Nepal."

"You brought mercenaries with you?"

"It's preferable to using the Sheik's Army for my immediate security. My father and mother were killed with help from the inside, Nikki, while the Sheik's Army was allegedly guarding them. I am not safe until I have learned who betrayed them."

"So your personal guards are the ones in the red turbans, with the different knives?"

"Kukri knives. In times past it was said that once a Gurkha drew a kukri in battle, it had to taste blood, or its owner had to cut himself before returning the blade to its sheath."

His warning was implicit—don't mess with my guards.

"And…these men are not worried about you being in here with me, alone?"

His voice lowered, dangerous. Sensual. "Should they be?"

The walls of the great hall suddenly felt too close. Her breathing quickened. "What…what about Omair?" she said, her voice thick. "Why not protect him?"

Zakir smiled again—not the arrogant flash that had lit his eyes and twisted her hormones into a hot soup earlier, but a warm smile that sneaked the softness of affection into his dark eyes. "Omair is the black sheep prince of our family. He's disappeared somewhere into the South American jungles. I've been unable to make contact with him. I doubt our enemies will find him, either. Not unless he chooses to be found. And then I'd worry—not for him, but the enemy."

Nikki detected genuine fondness, and frustration—a sense of family. She could relate. Family was everything to

Nikki. It was everything that had been taken from her that Christmas Eve. "What does Omair do for a living that he's in the jungle?" She paused. "Presuming he actually needs to make a living."

Zakir grinned and shrugged. "No one really knows."

Nikki sensed Zakir knew exactly what Omair did. Intrigue curled into her. She returned her attention to the portrait, her gaze sliding down to a more recent photograph of Tariq on the table beneath it. She bent forward suddenly, gripped by raw reflex as it hit her. *She knew him!*

Her eyes shot up to the painting, then back to the photograph. Blood began to pound in her ears.

She'd met Tariq. In her past life, at a medical convention in D.C. nine years ago, where she'd been a guest speaker, where he'd asked her questions about a very rare genetic ocular disorder. Irrational panic whipped through Nikki as thoughts of Sam crowded in on her.

Her mouth went dry, and she didn't dare turn around for fear of what her face might reveal to Zakir.

He came closer. Behind her. Sensing something. She could feel his height, his warmth. Her skin began to tingle. Fear. She couldn't breathe.

"That photo of Tariq was taken in Washington, D.C., about eight or nine years ago. Tariq is now a well-known neurosurgeon and geneticist. My father was very proud of him."

Nikki started to shake inside.

She couldn't look at Zakir. Something, she had to say something. "Very…interesting." But she choked on the words.

He touched her gently on her shoulder and she jumped. "Nikki, are you all right?"

Her hand shot to her chest. "I…I just need air. I'm tired.

I need to get some sleep." She started to move toward the door.

But he slid his hand down her arm, grasped her wrist. Gentle but firm, brooking no argument. "You are not going anywhere, Nikki. Please understand this. You are not free to leave. Now sit, have something to eat, have some wine."

"I already told you, I don't drink. Now please, let go of me!"

Little did he know she'd kill for a mind-numbing shot of vodka right now. But alcohol had almost killed her after the twins' deaths. At times she'd wished it had.

The only thing that had saved Nikki from taking her own life seven years ago had been finding Mercy Missions and a purpose in Africa. Where she could save other people's lost children after failing her own.

Zakir released her arm slowly, his gaze shifting inquiringly between Nikki and the photograph that had apparently spooked her. His features turned hard, suspicious. "Do you know Tariq, Nikki? You're originally from D.C., and you work in the medical profession. Perhaps you have met him?"

She felt her face grow hotter. "No, I have not. I…I was just born there. And I'm just a pediatric nurse. I never worked with the surgeons."

Silently, she cursed the irony that the deceased person whose identity she'd bought had also been born in D.C. That fraudulent passport was supposed to be her ticket to freedom. A way to hide from Sam and her own past. Now it could be her ticket to prison.

Her nursing papers and accreditation were fake, too.

And if Zakir found out she was a fraud, she could face extradition, lose her orphans. She *had* to get to them before he learned the truth of who she was.

He hooked his knuckle under her jaw, tilting her chin up,

forcing her to look into his eyes. "Nikki, if I find out that you are lying to me, about anything—"

"I'm not."

"I sincerely hope so, because if I learn that you are here under false pretenses, or that you have come to harm my family or my country, I will spare you no mercy. Because, Nikki," he said very quietly, his mouth coming closer to hers, his breath feathering her lips, "treachery in Al Na'Jar *must* be punished by execution. It is the law."

Chapter 4

Dawn had broken, but already the heat was blistering as Zakir waited in the palace courtyard for Nikki to appear. Soldiers lined the ancient turreted walls, black figures silhouetted against a harsh sky. The flag of Al Na'Jar snapped in the hot desert wind, but the direction of the wind had shifted and it was no longer thick with the red-gold sands of the Sahara. Today the sky above was eggshell-blue, clear as glass. It would grow whiter, almost colorless, during the next hours as the sun climbed to a fiery zenith. Desert temperatures would soar further.

Dogs moving like shadows at his side, Zakir paced in the shade under the arches, the bejeweled scimitar sheathed at his hip bumping gently against his thigh as he moved, the clip of his riding boots ringing out loud on stone. His armed Gurkhas stood with watchful black eyes, their features obscured by the cloth of their red turbans. Their galabiyas—or long white tunics—were cinched at the waist with leather belts from which their sheathed kukri knives hung. The men were also armed with semiautomatic weapons, and they remained strategically and subtly positioned between Zakir and the Sheik's Army soldiers at all times, watching for signs of treachery among the soldiers.

No one trusted anyone, and shadows lurked within shadows even under the starkly bright skies of the Sahara morning.

In the middle of the courtyard a convoy of black Humvees gleamed in the heat, drivers waiting inside as supplies were carried by palace staff over the flagstones toward them.

Impatient, Zakir checked his watch, then suddenly he spotted Nikki being escorted by guards down the sweeping black marble stairs. They were led by Alar, his mother's maid-in-waiting, who had been attending to the prisoner.

Zakir's heart quickened.

He stopped pacing and stood to face her, squaring his shoulders and hooking his hands behind his back. He inhaled deeply, lifting his chin as he watched her approach.

With approval he noted she was suitably dressed for her trip in a long dark skirt and white blouse with long sleeves. A midnight-blue scarf covered her hair and a translucent veil adorned with small crystal beads covered her nose and mouth. Similar pieces of crystal were sewn along the tops of the slippers she wore and the stones winked in the sunlight as she walked tall and confident toward him.

Her eyes were fixed exclusively on his, and as she came closer a thrill chased up Zakir's spine.

But while he enjoyed watching her, Zakir warned himself that the eyes of a deeply traditional people were also watching him. As were the eyes of his hidden enemies. When it came to courtship and the relations between a man and a woman, Al Na'Jar was a complex country, one where traditionalists still killed lovers over transgressions of protocol.

Even perceived missteps could result in death.

He needed to be seen to be observing these rules, at least until he was officially crowned.

He smiled. "Good morning, Nikki."

Averting her gaze, she bowed her head slightly, as Alar had no doubt told her would be a respectable form of greeting the king in public. But up close he saw that her face was frighteningly pale under her sunburn. Dark circles also rimmed her eyes. A pang of sympathy stabbed through Zakir.

"I trust you found everything in your chambers to your satisfaction during the night?"

She nodded slightly, mouth tight. And as she lifted her eyes to his, Zakir saw that they were an even more startling turquoise under the bright sunlight. In them he read a flicker of fear.

"You did not sleep, Nikki," he said gently. "You are worried?"

"For my children," she said crisply. "Am I free to leave now? Did my passport and papers check out?"

Zakir frowned. She appeared anxious about her credentials. But her passport had looked legitimate. And the Mercy Missions base on the Canary Islands had also verified that a nurse named Nikki Hunt had been stationed at their outpost in Mauritania. The staff said they'd lost contact with the camp after a rebel attack. So far her story had held.

Beyond this, Zakir had decided not to alert any U.S. authority—and by default, possibly the U.S. media—to the presence of an American in his land. It would make Nikki an attractive target to the insurgents, and thus a danger to Zakir and his country.

That, in turn, could jeopardize sensitive diplomatic talks down the road.

His goal now was to have her expeditiously escorted into the Rahm Hills, where she could minister to her children under the watch of a special Gurkha cadre. As soon as her orphans had been stabilized, his men would transport Nikki and her children to the coast and put them on a ship to Tenerife. End of problem.

Spy or not, she'd be out of his hair.

Yet a part of Zakir was suddenly reluctant to see her leave. He was marching such a solitary road in Al Na'Jar, where he could confide in no one. He was still grieving over the sudden and brutal loss of his parents and older brother, still struggling to come to terms with his unexpected role as king. And deep down he was afraid of the lonely darkness that lay ahead in his life because of his secret disability.

Nikki was a familiar connection with the ways of the West—and a tempting diversion.

"Yes," he finally answered. "Your papers appear to be in order, Nikki."

Her body sagged with such visible relief that Zakir's frown deepened. "You did not expect this?"

"No. Yes. I mean—" She cleared her throat quickly. "I'm just glad to be able to be going back to my children."

He handed her a clipboard with her list of supplies affixed to it, then gestured with a broad sweep of his arm to the waiting convoy of black Humvees. "Your supplies are being loaded as we speak. I have included gifts of food and cloth for the Berber clan on my behalf, and I have arranged for a cadre of my personal guards to escort you to the south end of the Red Valley at the base of the Rahm Hills. A small desert camp will be waiting there, along with camels, which are presently en route from a Sheik's Army base in the area. You will go into the hills on camel—obviously the area is unsuitable for vehicles. Once there you may do what you need to care for your children. My men will then transport all of you to the Port of Al Na'Jar, where a ship will be waiting to take you to Tenerife. We have contacted the Mercy Missions base and told them to expect you. You may make further contact with the mission from the port."

Her turquoise eyes widened, and under the translucent veil her lips formed a soft "oh" of disbelief. A smile tentatively dimpled her cheeks as it dawned on her that she really was free to go to her children, that Zakir had actually helped her and delivered on his promise. Her hand went to her chest. "Sheik Zakir," she whispered. "Thank you!"

A soft warmth spurted through Zakir's chest at the sight of her unguarded pleasure. For the first time in his life it wasn't jewels or a sports car that he'd used to buy a woman's smile. It was something so simple, so pure—it satisfied him beyond words to make her happy. He realized then that he'd lost touch with some core elements in his life, and her delight was shifting something profound inside him.

It made him want to know this woman better. It made him wonder why she'd had so little faith that he'd actually keep his word. And it made him wish—just for a moment—that she wasn't leaving.

"Come," he said gently, holding his hand out toward the Humvee convoy. "You can double-check the supplies against your list as they're being loaded."

Nikki quickly hooked back a strand of gold hair that had escaped her scarf, and she got to work checking the Arabic labels on the boxes. Her movements were swift, efficient, focused on her task. As her long skirt swished about her legs and the sun danced off the crystal beads on her veil, Zakir couldn't help but watch her with increasing fascination. This job of saving orphans seemed to define Nikki—threaten her children and she became fearless. Offer to help them and she glowed.

Yet he'd glimpsed fear in her eyes.

As he watched her skirt sway about her legs, he felt a sudden surge of desire. He shook himself. This was absurd, wrong.

Yet there was something so seductively mysterious about this intriguing woman covered with veils, the promise inherent in the swirl of her skirt. He was finding it incredibly—and disturbingly—sexy.

She checked the last of the supplies off her list and glanced up, eyes now alive with turquoise fire, her skin luminous in the steadily climbing temperatures. "It's all here."

A Humvee door opened as she spoke, and the driver's-side mirror caught a flash of sunlight, bouncing it sharply across his face. Zakir blinked, momentarily blinded by the sudden glare. But while vision quickly returned to his right eye, a dark blurry circle lingered in the middle of his left.

His heart stalled.

Nikki came up to him and held out the clipboard. "Can I have my passport and papers back now?"

He reached for the clipboard, trying to pull focus back into his left eye, but the circle of darkness seemed to be expanding. Perspiration prickled over his skin as he struggled to maintain control. "My men will hold your papers until you reach the port," he said, turning his head sideways so that she fell at the periphery of his vision where he could see her better.

"Why?"

He heard the uneasiness in her voice. "In case you don't cooperate."

"So I'm still a prisoner?"

"A guest, under my protection. Be grateful, not angered, by my generosity, Ms. Hunt." He spun round to leave, desperate to get back into the palace where he could be alone, lie down and close his eyes to see if the vision returned. But the driver closed his door and again the mirror flashed a sharp burst of light into his eyes. Suddenly Zakir couldn't see a damn thing at all.

Panic slammed through him.

He stepped back quickly, reaching out to brace his palm

against the vehicle, metal searing hot under his skin. Staring fiercely, sightlessly ahead, he groped with his free hand alongside his thigh for Ghorab, but while talking to Nikki he'd moved around the Humvee without calling his tallest hound to his side. Tension squeezed his chest as he realized that Ghorab was not there the first time he really needed him.

Zakir clicked his fingers softly, and then suddenly he felt the damp nose of his saluki nudging into his palm.

Relief flooded through him as the connection with his dog steadied him slightly. But a new wave of anxiety overcame him. Could his men see what was happening to him? If they could—if the King's Council got wind of Zakir's problem before he was sworn in—his throne would be challenged and his kingdom would fall. Hundreds of years of Al Arif rule would be over because of him. Because of a weakness he could not control.

Suddenly, he felt Nikki's hand, cool and soft on his forearm. There was something reassuring about her touch, and as he breathed in deeply and his heartbeat calmed he found his vision slowly returning to his right eye.

But his left remained sightless.

Zakir realized he was wet with perspiration under his tunic. He glanced around the courtyard with his barely functional eye. Everything appeared to be moving normally—palace staff loading a case of clothes, his soldiers patrolling the turrets... the complete darkness must have lasted a mere nanosecond, but to Zakir it felt like an eternity.

Feigning anger, he quickly grasped Nikki's arm and pulled her around the side of the vehicle.

Nikki stiffened in confusion. "What are you doing—"

"Quiet," he growled, waving his bodyguards away as they tried to reposition between him and the Sheik's Army soldiers.

There was a chance the only person who had witnessed him falter was Nikki Hunt. And he had to control the damage.

Blood thudded in his ears as he tried to focus on her with his right eye, but his central vision in that one was still extremely blurry. And she was scrutinizing his eyes intently, looking into the very heart of his secret. Zakir blinked as another shaft of reflected sunlight glanced off a sword as his guards retreated.

Her hand touched his forearm again, and she came very close to him. "Are you all right, Zakir?" she whispered, out of earshot of his men.

"I'm fine." He glowered at her hand. A female touching him like this in public was inappropriate, a very wrong message to send to his staff, his people.

She retracted her hand quickly. "I…I'm sorry. You looked like you blacked out for a moment."

He cast his eyes down, spoke quietly, angrily. "Before I can let you go, Nikki, there is something you have not explained to my satisfaction. Tell me why the Rahm Berbers did not kill you on sight? What made them trust you?"

Zakir's mind raced wildly as he spoke. The vision in his right eye was improving in increments, but his left eye remained blind. This was a terrible shock. This was not supposed to happen for at least another twelve months, according to Tariq. He needed to speak to his brother, find out if there was a treatment to prolong vision loss. But he couldn't use the palace phones, nor could he consult with a royal physician. The risk of exposure was too great.

Zakir feared another episode like this could hit at any second, any hour. Any day. And it when it did, the periods of darkness would start coming closer and closer together until one final episode would leave him completely blind, permanently. His mouth turned dry. He could not let that happen, not until he was officially sworn in as king.

Nikki's attention was still riveted on Zakir's eyes. "I am not some kind of spy for the Rahm tribesmen, or for anyone else, Zakir. They let me live for the same reason your soldiers didn't shoot me in the street. I am a humanitarian worker ~~who~~—"

"Nikki," he said very quietly, feigning complete calm as he desperately tried to bring her features into focus. "Those tribesmen are aggressive—they never ask questions first. They would've slit the throat of a strange-looking Tuareg crossing into their territory on sight. Yet they did not. And I want to know the reason."

"I encountered an elderly Rahm shepherd in the desert," she said, still watching his eyes. "He'd fallen, gashed his head on a rock and was unconscious. After reviving him I cleaned and bandaged his wound, gave him the last of our water and we got him up onto my camel. He told me how to take him to his village in the mountains, and we did," she said. "If I hadn't come across him, he would've died."

"So you saved the old man's life, and in return for the favor the shepherd's family was willing to protect your orphans?"

"That's correct."

"And this is when they told you about the coup?"

"Yes. They told me that they call you the Dark King."

His jaw tightened at the irony. The Dark King, destined for a future of darkness…little did they know.

"And they warned me to be very careful, that you could be dangerous…." She hesitated, as if weighing whether to speak the next words.

"All of it," he demanded. "Tell me *everything* they said."

She inhaled deeply. "They said you might have orchestrated the coup yourself, using elements in your father's military."

"So that's why you accused me of doing this?"

"The Berbers fear the legacy your rule might bring, Zakir. They know nothing about you because you have been living abroad."

Her words sparked a frenzy of ideas in his mind, and suddenly Zakir knew what he must do—how he could hide from the members of the King's Council until he could come up with a strategy to deal with his rapidly failing vision. He also needed to contact his emissary in Europe to hasten the search for a wife. He *had* to marry before he lost his sight.

"I'm coming to the Rahm Hills with you," he stated. "I will meet with the tribesmen, speak to them myself. Since you've earned their trust, you will introduce me, be an escort to me and my men."

After he'd met with the sheik of the Berber village, Zakir and a few of his Gurkhas could continue on to the Al Arif Summer Palace, not far from the Rahm range. It would be an ideal place to lie low while he arranged his marriage.

The palace had traditionally served as a refuge for the royal family during the hot summer months. Situated high in the north mountains, it was well fortified, and it enjoyed the cooler winds that blew up from the Atlantic. It also had a much smaller staff.

He could govern from there for a short while, using envoys and telecommunications. He'd send for more security personnel and inform his Council once he'd arrived.

He raised his hand high in the air, snapping his fingers sharply, and his secretary rushed to his side. "Change of plan," he said. "I will personally accompany Ms. Hunt into the Rahm Hills. Repack the supplies from the royal Humvee fleet into two camouflaged army vehicles. I want to travel under the radar. I will take only my top five trusted bodyguards."

Zakir spun away from Nikki, barking further orders in rapid-fire Arabic. Staff, guards, soldiers scattered in all directions as if he'd kicked an ant heap. He donned a pair of sunglasses handed to him by an aide as a modified military Humvee drew into the courtyard, followed by a second one. Both were the color of desert sand and shadows. The aide opened the door of the first vehicle, and Zakir gestured to the backseat. "Please get in, Nikki."

She hesitated, watching Zakir with interest. Nikki had just witnessed him stumble and grasp for his dog. Then when a shaft of reflected sunlight had moved across his eyes, Nikki saw what she knew as a Marcus Gunn pupil—a pupillary defect indicating a lack of response to light in his left eye.

She knew eyes intimately—she'd been a top ophthalmic surgeon.

A normal response to bright light would be equal constriction of both pupils. Zakir clearly had some kind of damage to the optic nerve of his left eye and quite possibly his right as well, judging by the way he'd then stumbled, as if totally blinded for a moment.

She thought again of Dr. Tariq Al Arif and the very specific questions he'd asked after at that medical convention nine years ago. The conversation had stuck in Nikki's mind because of his interest in a very rare hereditary disorder called Naveed's Hereditary Optic Neuropathy—named after Dr. Anwar Naveed, the Iranian-born German ophthalmologist who first described the condition.

This genetic disorder was passed only through a mother's DNA, but the degeneration of retinal ganglion cells and their axons affected only males and only one or two men every couple of generations. The disease was also unique to families of Moorish or Bedouin lineage.

Dr. Al Arif had told Nikki that his own family carried this rare gene, and he hoped to one day be able to cure the hereditary ailment with genetic surgery *before* any onset of vision loss. He'd asked for her input on identifying markers following her speech on Leber's hereditary optic neuropathy, a related condition. Worried that the blindness was due to resurface in his generation, he thought if he could find the right genetic markers he'd be able to detect who carried the disease well before it manifested itself. And that was the point he believed it could be treated—and blindness prevented.

Her pulse raced as she put two and two together.

Nikki thought of the candlelight in the dining hall and how in that low and quavering light Zakir had angled his head slightly to the side whenever he'd spoken to her, a sign that his central vision was diminishing.

She thought of the list she'd handed him and how he wouldn't read it. How his dogs were always at his side. And it hit her with a jolt.

Sheik Zakir was going blind.

And if Nikki was right, if Zakir did indeed have Naveed's Hereditary Optic Neuropathy, judging by his pupillary reaction, he'd already entered the acute stage of the genetic disorder. If so, he was going to have more of these episodes, each coming closer and closer together.

One of them would be permanent.

And by the way the king had manhandled her behind the car, it was a secret he didn't want anyone to know.

Chapter 5

Moments later they were speeding out of the massive palace gates and down the palm-lined boulevard, just one more military sortie in a city besieged by unrest. Nikki sat with Zakir and Ghorab behind tinted, bulletproof windows in the military vehicle taking up the rear. One of his Gurkhas drove, a second guard besides him with a machine gun. Zakir's other hounds traveled in the leading Humvee with three more bodyguards.

Soldiers scrambled under the burning sun to haul back the cordon of razor wire across the boulevard, and once through the blockade, the Humvee convoy accelerated, racing bumper to bumper through the dusty and ancient city.

Nikki held her hands tensely in her lap as she watched the scenery fly by—high walls of historic medinas, shimmering domes and minarets of mosques, the occasional glittering Mercedes-Benz vying for road space with rattling old trucks, donkeys that labored in front of wooden carts, and women drifting like silent black ghosts in burkas while others wore brightly patterned African cloth and elaborately folded head-dresses.

For a shining nanosecond she'd thought she was free, that she and her kids would be on their way.

Now she was trapped with the Dark King himself in a bulletproof cocoon, hurtling through an ancient desert city toward the barren and ominous Rahm Hills. And he still had her passport.

Nikki stole a sidelong glance at his arrogant profile.

His thick blue-black hair had been pulled back into a ponytail, accentuating the high bridge of his nose, the thrust of his cheekbones. He looked undeniably regal, powerful—almost dangerously so, like a dark jungle cat, relaxed yet ready to attack like lightning.

His eyes, however, were now masked by black shades. His hand rested on the sleek head of Ghorab, as if the hound was feeding the king's power, his confidence. Nikki couldn't stop an unbidden empathy from stirring into her tightening sense of claustrophobia.

She'd seen how urgently he'd groped for that dog, how his entire body had relaxed as he felt the saluki's snout nuzzle into his hand.

If Nikki's guess about his condition was correct, even the slightest amount of stress would hasten vision loss. Any increase in blood pressure would place additional strain on the degenerating optic nerves.

The man needed to relax, and his new role as leader of a country in crisis was not going to allow him to do that. Nikki could recommend antihypertensive medication that would help mitigate the pressure on his nerves and prolong visual acuity. But giving Zakir this information would mean revealing her true identity.

Her hands knotted more tightly in her lap.

His health is not my business. What I've done is illegal. Telling him could bring Sam back into my life.

Zakir's threat also snaked through her mind. *If I learn that you are here under false pretenses, I will be able to spare you no mercy. Treachery in Al Na'Jar must be punished by execution.*

Nikki shot another glance at Zakir. Was he capable of making that kind of example of her?

Who was Sheik Zakir Al Arif, really, under that powerful exterior? A man in trouble himself? He *had* to be afraid of what lay ahead, if her diagnosis was correct. She'd dealt with patients losing sight. She knew the range of emotions they went through.

He caught her watching him, and Nikki glanced away quickly, mouth dry. Yet another worry was mushrooming inside her—one sprouted by Zakir's comments about murderous Rahm Berbers.

Nikki had seen the fear and aggression in their eyes when they'd spoken about the Dark King. Now here she was bringing the ruler himself—along with armed guards—right into their remote and hidden mountain village. Their trust in Nikki might be shattered. The Berbers might no longer feel obliged to protect her orphans.

She needed to go into those hills alone, first, and talk to them, pave the way for Zakir's convoy.

"Zakir," she said quietly, "why is it so important for you to meet with the Rahm tribesmen so suddenly?"

He regarded her in silence for several beats, his features implacable, a dark kinetic energy rolling from him in waves. "It is not your place to question me." Leaning forward he slammed the tinted window between them and the guards shut with a thud.

Nikki frowned inwardly. Zakir didn't want his men to hear

her question him. Nor had he wanted his men to see him stumble.

He wanted to appear powerful, in control. He wore his dark autocracy like his brocade tunic—over everything else, for all to see. He projected his alpha control with each powerful stride of his boots, the arrogant tilt of his jaw, the square set of his shoulders, the way he rested his hand on the bejeweled hilt of his scimitar.

But what lay underneath?

Was he like her husband—a narcissistic and dangerous tyrant at heart, a man capable of hiring a killer to run her off an icy road?

Zakir caught her studying him, and heat flushed her cheeks. Nikki turned to peer out the window. But she could feel Zakir scrutinizing her from behind, and her whole body heated further—a combination of adrenaline, fear and a very disturbing reawakening of her own femininity.

Nikki's pulse began to race.

Her own buried sexuality was the last place on earth Nikki intended to revisit. It made her uncomfortable. Brought the past too close to the present. Brought too many painful memories.

Her jaw tightened and her eyes burned as she struggled to shut down the sensations simmering to life inside her.

Buildings appeared more sparsely now—flat desert adobes with melons and white pumpkins weighing down tin roofs. A small oasis of palms sprouted out of sand, and then there was nothing as the scenery blurred into a softly undulating sea of gold dunes that stretched as far as the eye could see. And in the distance loomed the jagged outline of the Rahm Hills.

The wind was shifting again, lifting spindrift off the dunes and fanning waves of sand across the road. Tension tightened in Nikki's chest as the ragged mountains loomed closer.

Zakir turned to her suddenly. "Was this the way you traveled into Na'Jar?"

She moistened her lips, nodded. "It took two days by camel to reach the city from the Rahm Hills." She forced a smile. "Seems odd to now be flying along in air-conditioned comfort."

He nodded. "Cut off from the tactile sensations of the desert—the endless silence, the feel of the wind against your face, the heat beating down on your head."

Nikki raised her brows, but Zakir said nothing more. Outside, the harmattan whipped harder. Sand began to tick and scrape against the windows, trying to find a way in.

"Tell me again, Nikki," he said suddenly, turning to face her. "How was it that you were able to cross the Sahara, especially at this time of year? How did you find the mental fortitude to stay the course when so many would give up and die?"

He revealed nothing in his tone, and Nikki couldn't read his eyes behind the black shades. But she sensed he was testing her.

She also knew how easily she *could* have given up in that ocean of burning sand. The unnatural silence followed by the sudden, inhuman scream of a sandstorm; the shifting sense of time; the continuous thirst and hunger. The scorching heat. It had played havoc with her mind. It had been one of the toughest things she'd ever done.

"I had my children," she said.

"It's that simple?"

"I could never abandon them, Zakir. Those orphans have nothing left in this world—except me."

"And what will happen to them once they reach the mission base on Tenerife?"

"With proper food and care they'll grow strong. They'll have a chance to experience a childhood they've never known.

And perhaps some will be lucky and adopted." She adjusted her veil as she spoke, feeling uncomfortable. She'd been so focused on just staying alive, getting her kids to Tenerife that she hadn't managed to picture life beyond that. And it suddenly made her feel lost to think about it. What would *she* do then? Return to another mission outpost, start over?

"And Samira," she continued, "the fourteen-year-old, will be able to give birth to a child who'll at least have a fighting chance of survival." Her voice caught as she thought of Samira and her baby. Nikki desperately wanted to show the young girl that beauty could still grow from the horrors of war.

That there *was* hope in this world.

She needed to see this herself. It was why it was so fundamentally important for Nikki to get Samira to safety.

Zakir frowned inwardly, his interest in Nikki deepening.

"You know," she said, her voice growing distant, "there were times out in that desert when I thought we weren't going to make it, and oddly that's exactly when the desert would reveal its beauty to me. And suddenly life was worth fighting for again. The same desert that was breaking me would also renew my strength." She paused. "I felt free out there. Part of me…just wanted to stay there."

Zakir felt pleasure curve his lips, and a sense of kinship warmed his chest. Nikki's almost poetic love of the Sahara tapped into a part of himself he'd buried when he'd moved to Europe.

She was an enigma, a woman with incredible courage, determination and beauty.

Yet for all these reasons suspicion continued to waltz softly arm in arm with his growing attraction to Nikki. He'd been burned by a woman like her. A woman he'd taken into his bed and his heart. A woman he'd trusted and very nearly married.

It wasn't a mistake he would make again.

Nikki had also seen him stumble. He needed to be careful. Zakir wanted to expose nothing more to her before she left this country, or she would definitely become a liability to him at this very delicate time.

As they entered the Red Valley, the wind sucked fiercely through a gorge, churning up a maelstrom of sand that hissed like rough static. The vehicles began to rock. Nikki peered through the blur until suddenly she recognized the silhouette of an immense red sandstone structure that had been sharpened by relentlessly scouring winds into the shape of giant swords.

Her heart kicked.

The Rahm tribesmen called it the Rock of Swords. From its base several mountain paths ran off in various directions.

Zakir was going to ask her which path to take.

If there were Rahm sentinels watching from higher up, and if they saw this military convoy entering their territory, her kids could be doomed. She had to stop Zakir here. She had to convince him to let her go alone from this point.

"Stop. This is the spot."

Zakir rapped on the window behind his driver, motioning for him to halt the convoy. The man radioed the other Humvee. It rolled to a stop.

"Which is the path to the village?" asked Zakir.

"I…I need to get out and check," she said, grasping for the door handle. If there were Berber sentinels out there, Nikki wanted them to see it was her inside this Humvee. But the door was locked. Urgency tore through her.

"Please, let me out, quick."

He frowned. "I'll tell the driver to take us closer."

"No. I need to walk. It'll help me remember," she lied. "Things look different from inside a vehicle."

He got out himself and came around to open her door, wind whipping his tunic.

His men were also exiting the other vehicle, positioning strategically, their machine guns and AK-47s at the ready. Tension crackled in the wind around them, hot, restless, shifting, hungry. The tiny crystal beads that fringed the base of Nikki's veil flicked sharply against her neck.

"I'm going to take a look," she called over the wind. Clutching her headscarf about her face, Nikki leaned into the maelstrom. Her long skirt snapped about her ankles as she began to make her way toward the Rock of Swords.

Zakir stayed right by her side. It made her nervous. If Berber sentinels recognized him, they might mistrust her intentions. She had to make it clear that the king and his Gurkhas could not cross beyond the Rock of Swords.

As they neared the haunting geological formation, the wind moaned eerily through the cavities, and Nikki's gauzy veil was suddenly snatched loose by a sharp eddy. It fluttered up, disappearing into the cloud of yellow sand.

She pulled her headscarf across the side of her face as she huddled back into a protected lee formed by the rocks. She had to tell him, now.

"I...I need to go into the mountains alone, Zakir." The wind snatched at her words, tossing them down the Red Valley in a swirl of sand.

"What did you say?" He came closer, bending his head toward her.

Determination bit into her. "I said I must go alone to the village," she yelled over the roar of sand. "Without you or your men!"

Through the blur of sand, Nikki could see his bodyguards edging closer like wraiths, trying to keep their king in their sights. Zakir waved them back angrily and his fingers dug into her upper arm as he trapped her against the sandstone. "What in hell are you trying to do?"

"If the Berbers see you approaching with armed soldiers

they'll think I betrayed them, Zakir. Like you said, they don't ask questions first. My children could be hurt."

"I am their king. I *must* speak with them."

"Zakir, please. Let me go alone first. I will explain why you're here, pave the way for you. *Then* you and your men can come in."

She sensed the energy of his guards shifting and they began to close in again.

Furiously staying his guards for a second time, Zakir's expression darkened. He swore in Arabic, tightening his grip on her arm. "Just get back in the vehicle, Nikki," he growled, voice low, dangerous.

Nikki tried to resist, but Zakir's strength was phenomenal as he brusquely dragged her back toward the Humvee. He swung open the door and manhandled her into the backseat so hard and fast that it shocked her. No man had touched her like this since Sam, and Nikki reacted instinctively—violently— fighting back and kicking at him.

Which enraged Zakir further.

He forced her down onto the seat and climbed in after her, slamming the door closed behind him. His guards stood outside, unable to see in.

He was breathing hard. His body was pressed on top of hers, their hearts beating in angry unison. Sweat dampened her skin and grit stuck to it. He lowered his mouth, almost touching hers. "Don't *ever* disobey or challenge me in public," he growled. "Understand?"

She was furious, unable to breathe under his weight, but the sensation of his hard body against hers awakened a whole other kind of panic. As did the sensation of his warm breath over her lips. Nikki hadn't felt a man's weight on top of her in seven years and desire tore through her, so hot and fast and sudden that she began to shake.

He ripped off his glasses, obsidian eyes tunneling fiercely

into hers as if to negate the weakness she'd glimpsed earlier. To show he was still strong. In command.

Her heart lodged in her throat at his raw intensity. And fear whispered. Would he hurt her like Sam had? Her husband had gone so far as to hire someone to kill her—but the hired gun had killed her children by mistake.

When Zakir finally spoke, his voice was pure steel. "You *will* obey my word or our deal is off. No medicine. No safe passage. Instead I will return you to Al Na'Jar and ship you off to the States in one of my jets."

Terror lashed through her. She could not lose her orphans. She could *never* return to the States.

"How *dare* you threaten me," she ground out. "How dare you hold innocent children hostage for your own royal pride!"

"It's not pride, Nikki," he whispered angrily, so close she could feel the beating of his heart. "Allowing a woman to undermine my authority in public is sacrilegious. If it got back to the Council that I permitted a woman to touch me—a woman to whom I am not betrothed—my throne *will* be challenged. And I *will* lose. Don't do this again, Nikki, or I will be forced protect my country over helping you."

"You mean protect your power," she said angrily.

His eyes burned into hers. "My power, Nikki—" his voice went lower "—is the *only* way I can protect my people and honor my family and my father's will. This is my duty, my only obligation."

She swallowed, face flushing. And with alarm she realized her blouse button had popped open in their tussle, exposing the lace of her bra. Nikki's gaze slid in horror down to her exposed chest.

Zakir followed her gaze. He was silent for a moment, then his eyes lifted, met hers. And in that instant they both felt the intensity of the sexual chemistry between them, fired by adrenaline. He swallowed, but barely missed a beat. "Now tell me which is the path to the Berber village."

"Zakir, I understand your constraints. But I just cannot risk the lives of my children by allowing the Berbers to think I betrayed them by bringing you and your soldiers into their hidden village." Her voice quavered slightly, but she stuck to her guns. Never again would a man push her around. Never again would some alpha tyrant take her children. "If you don't let me go alone," she said, "I won't go at all."

His features turned hawkish, dangerous. "You think *you* can issue *me* an ultimatum?"

Nikki began to shake inside, but swallowed her fear. "I just did," she whispered.

Chapter 6

She was serious.

If there was one thing Zakir had learned in both business and pleasure, it was never to put into a corner a man—or woman—who had absolutely nothing left to lose.

He sat up slowly, smoothed his palm over his hair.

She wriggled into a sitting position, angrily yanking her blouse back over her bra. But as she did, her scarf caught behind her and pulled off her hair. And Zakir's focus was shot.

Her tousled strawberry-gold curls, the shape of her mouth, the rapid rise and fall of her chest completely stole his attention and ability to reason. An urge to reach out, touch her hair, feel those silky curls between his fingers overcame him.

And Zakir knew he was in trouble. The only way he was going to get rid of this growing compulsion to touch Nikki Hunt was to get her out of his sight. Out of his country. Out of his mind.

And one way to accomplish that was to get this visit to

the Berbers over with stat. Then he could go in peace to his Summer Palace, where his next worry would be to find a wife.

"Think about it, Zakir," she said crisply as she re-covered her hair with her scarf. He noticed her hands were trembling. "The Berber tribesmen have scouts everywhere in these hills. They'll see us coming from miles away, and your convoy will meet resistance. Trust me on this, if—"

"Trust *you?* On matters of my own country and people?" He laughed condescendingly. "Do you honestly think I do not have contingency plans for the possibility of an ambush when we enter those hills?"

"That's the last situation you want. You could lose hold of the Rahm Hills if you go in there and start up a war."

Zakir felt irked by her challenge, yet he was increasingly surprised by this woman's boldness—and his confounding attraction to her. "That, Nikki," he said patronizingly, "is why I came here with you. To meet with the sheik of this clan and talk to his people."

She leaned forward, pressing her point. "And that, Zakir, is exactly why you *must* let me go to their village alone. Please, let me be your envoy. Let me secure my children, and *then* you and your men can come in."

Zakir exhaled in frustration. She was right, and he knew it. She was astute and an incredibly fast read of a situation.

And truthfully, Zakir had not considered the well-being of her orphans. He'd been wholly focused on politics, on saving his country. Wasn't that more important?

Perhaps the children didn't even exist.

Perhaps this woman had ulterior motives.

Zakir cursed in Arabic and dragged his hand over his hair again.

She was also the kind of woman he could use on his side. Nikki understood tribal cultures. She spoke Arabic. She loved the desert. She had sharp political insight, and she was bold. She was also a link to the Western life Zakir had grown accustomed to, a lifestyle he'd enjoyed.

In some ways Nikki was a lot like him—her feet planted in two different worlds. A bridge between two cultures. Never mind the fact she was also beautiful and incredibly desirable.

Zakir shook himself, feeling light-headed, then suddenly he realized his vision was blurring again. He reached quickly for his sunglasses. "Fine," he said quietly, his mind racing. "We'll compromise. My men will stay in the Red Valley while I go alone with you to meet the Berbers."

She considered his proposal. "You'll go unarmed?"

"No. That I cannot do." *Because I have yet to trust you.*

She opened her mouth to protest, but he raised his hand. "I will, however, travel in the robes of a simple Berber. If they see us approaching from afar, I will merely look like your guide. When we meet them, you can explain your 'guest.' Your children will not come to harm this way, Nikki."

"But when they learn it is *you?*"

"By then I will be in their custody, in their village. I will not be a threat to them. They will be in control."

She studied him, something akin to respect crossing her features. Clearly, she had not expected this of him. And in spite of himself, Zakir liked the way it felt to surprise her, to win her respect.

Silence hung for several beats. "All right," she said quietly.

"Wait here," he commanded.

Zakir got out of the Humvee, called Ghorab to his side and stood motionless in the wind for a second, his hand resting on his dog as he considered his next steps. And as his blood pressure eased, so did the dark blur in his left eye. He noted this. It was something he needed to tell Tariq as soon as possible.

Zakir then strode over to Tenzing Gelu, his lead bodyguard, the man he trusted most. "We're going to the base camp at the south end of the Red Valley. The Sheik's Army camel handler should be waiting there with animals by now. You will all remain at the camp while Ms. Hunt and I travel ahead on camel to meet the Berbers," he said brusquely. "We will remain in radio contact at all times, and I will carry a GPS so that you can map the way into their village."

A ripple of surprise passed through the guard and his men. They were his top five bodyguards, and they knew he was taking a risk. "May I speak, your Royal Highness?" asked Gelu.

"Make it quick. I want to get into those mountains before nightfall."

"I do not believe this is wise, your Highness. You could meet with an ambush. The woman herself is not to be trusted. She could be allied to the enemy."

"I am aware of this," he snapped. "I will watch her carefully. And I will be armed. She will not."

"But your Highness—"

He raised his hand. "Enough. We move. Now!"

Gelu caught the eyes of the other guards, but no one said anything more.

Zakir paced beneath the Bedouin tent cover, his boots soundless on the soft sand. The small desert encampment at the south end of the Red Valley provided only minimal respite from the windstorm. A table with monitoring and radio equipment had been set up under the canvas, behind a screen. With this equipment his Gurkha militia would track his progress into the mountains.

He'd sent Nikki to wait in another tent while he changed

his robes and organized the loading of supplies onto camels. Zakir had already dismissed the animals' handler and sent him back to his camp. He did not want anyone from the army aware of his new plans. He trusted only his Gurkhas.

It's better to die than to be a coward.

That was the historic slogan of the Gurkhas—Nepalese soldiers once designated by the Victorian British as having been descended from a "martial race." The British military still recruited about 200 Gurkhas each year in one of the toughest and most fiercely contested military selection procedures in the world.

Omair had informed Zakir that 30,000 young men vied for the British Army spots each year, and the private military company for which Omair contracted had managed to start recruiting several hundred of these Gurkhas annually—men who'd either been overlooked in the selection process or soldiers who had chosen to retire from the ranks of the British military. Tenzing Gelu was such a man. He had a long history with the Brits, but had chosen to leave in favor of a more lucrative freelance profession.

Omair had personally selected a cadre of these Gurkhas for Zakir's protection after the assassination of their parents and brother, and he'd put them through a rapid Arabic learning process, which was still ongoing.

Zakir's Gurkhas had no emotional or historical connection to the locals of Al Na'Jar and would be loyal only to him for the duration of their contract.

While Zakir had told Nikki that he knew little of Omair's movements, it was only partially true. Omair remained in constant contact with his brothers even though the exact nature of his whereabouts was kept secret. Omair could just as easily be deep in some South American jungle as he could be moving undercover among the top society of Washington, D.C., or in London.

But one thing Zakir did know was that once Omair had taken on a mission he'd stop at nothing until his jambiya had tasted the blood of his quarry.

Zakir flicked out his wrist and checked his watch. He wanted to leave within the next ten minutes.

The canvas walls of her tent flapped in gusts, and sand scraped at the outsides. Nerves danced inside Nikki's stomach. Would she remember the way into the village? It all seemed so different in the blowing sand.

She plunked down onto the military camp cot and began running through the landmarks in her mind, but suddenly something in the atmosphere shifted and the hair on the back of her neck prickled—someone had entered the tent.

But before she could spin around, a cold blade pressed against her throat and a hand clamped over mouth, skin rough, dry. "Do not make a sound," a man's voice hissed in her ear in English.

She nodded slightly, afraid that any movement would cause the knife to slice into her skin. And slowly it dawned on her—it was the long edge of a kukri blade that was being held at her throat.

Gradually the man eased pressure of the blade, came around to face her, a finger on his lips reminding her to remain silent. Shock raced through her as she recognized Zakir's lead Gurkha.

Tenzing Gelu.

"Listen carefully," he said, blade still under her throat. Sweat began to prickle over her lip.

"You'll be the only one with his Royal Highness for the next two days, possibly more," he said quietly, in perfect English. "You will watch the king's every move and report back to me when you return. I need to know exactly what the king says to the Berbers, what promises he makes them. I want to know the names of the men he talks to. I want to know what those men tell the king of their alliances with other tribes in the region. Everything. And you will not breathe one word of this to him."

"What on earth makes you think I will agree to do this?" she whispered.

"If you don't, your children will die."

She quieted, glancing at the tent entrance, a new kind of fear rising in her.

"If I even think you have breathed a word of this to the king, not even he will be able to protect your orphans."

"I don't believe you," she hissed.

Sand whipped the tent flap, sending it clapping against the side panel.

He bent close, his breath bitter, the kukri pressing tighter against her throat.

"Are you ready to gamble with their lives—the fourteen-year-old's in particular? Because I will start with her."

She swallowed, bitter bile and hatred rising in her throat. She glared at the man's eyes and saw no emotion at all. How did he know about Samira? Then it hit her—he'd been one of the guards who dragged her from Zakir's chambers. He'd have heard Nikki's desperate plea to the king. He knew just how much Samira meant to her.

"Why are you doing this? You're not even from Al Na'Jar," she said, voice low, eyes crackling, fear racing with growing rage. "This is not your country. This is not your political battle. What's in this for you?"

He smiled, one side of his mouth curving a little higher. His teeth were in a perfect white row, small. "I'm a mercenary, Ms. Hunt. I work for the highest bidder."

"Who is that bidder?"

He laughed softly, but with no light in his eyes. And she was scared.

"I'll expect that report when you return."

Nikki glared at him, shaking inside. The man removed the blade from her throat and backed out of her tent.

Zakir handed Nikki a camel rope. She took it with her right hand, where he'd noticed the calluses. Clucking her tongue, she coaxed the animal to lower itself to the ground and climbed expertly into the saddle, clicking her tongue again. The camel protested, pulling back its lips and showing yellowed teeth, yet she managed to make it rise like a complaining wobbly leviathan. Zakir repressed a small smile.

He felt a grudging admiration for the way she'd stuck to her guns in arguing with him.

He also liked the way she'd felt under him. But he quashed that thought. "Ready?" he called to her over the wind.

She nodded, looking a little pale.

Zakir frowned. Every now and then he felt in his gut she was telling the truth. But then there were signs that once again made him nervous. He'd have to watch her carefully.

He mounted his own camel and flicked his tasseled whip, calling his dogs to heel behind him, and they began to move in a small convoy. Zakir allowed Nikki to take the lead so he could watch her back. A third camel, roped to his, took up the rear with the medical supplies and gifts for the Berbers, along with ropes and tent equipment.

The wind grew harsh as they neared the Rock of Swords. Zakir wound his kaffiyeh over his nose and mouth to keep the dust out. His eyes were hidden behind shades. He looked like an ordinary Berber dressed in plain black, riding his camel.

Nikki also wound her scarf like a turban over her face and hunched into the hot wind.

They rounded the Rock of Swords and began to climb a very narrow and steep path into the mountains.

Chapter 7

Nikki squinted into the wind, her knuckles white as she gripped her camel rope. She'd lost track of how many hours they'd been climbing. The trail had narrowed, a chasm dropping sharply off to her left, the blowing sand obscuring her vision of the cliff edge.

As they climbed higher into the mountains, clouds began to roll over the jagged peaks, sweeping down over them in great big tatters, worsening visibility. She wondered if Zakir could see much in this light. But as she turned to glance back at him, her camel lost its footing and stumbled. Nikki gasped as dislodged stones and rocks clattered down into the void on her left. She reined in her camel, heart thudding.

Had she lost the way? Taken the wrong path?

Zakir came up behind her, his dogs following him in single file along the very narrow trail. "You sure this is the right trail?" he called over the wind.

"I…I think so. It's hard to make out the landmarks in this storm."

"It'll be dark soon. We won't be able to travel without light from the moon or stars tonight. We need to find a place to set up camp."

He was wearing his long wool cape now to ward off the chill at this high elevation. She, too, wore a cape that had been packed for her at the palace, and she was grateful for the warmth. But in spite of his simple black garb, Zakir could not hide his regal stature. He looked like a man born to lead whether in common turban and cloak on a camel or in glittering brocade in his castle.

His words snaked through her mind. *I have enemies who will not stop until they have wiped out the entire Al Arif bloodline. They are bold and highly creative.*

It was true. More so than he realized. His enemy lurked among his most trusted bodyguards. She should tell him.

But she didn't doubt the intent in that Gurkha's eyes. There was something reptilian about Tenzing Gelu that chilled her soul. She believed he'd follow through on his threat.

Nikki had to think of her kids first. This was not her country—or battle.

Or was it?

Had Tenzing Gelu just made it hers? She closed her eyes for a moment, feeling trapped.

"Nikki?"

Her eyes flared open. "I'm fine." She clucked her tongue quickly and nudged her camel forward. Slowly, they began to climb again, the path growing narrower, steeper, closer to the cliff edge.

Nikki topped a rise, and suddenly the sky was clear again. At this elevation, they were above the blizzard of sand being whipped across the valley and foothills below. But even though the wind carried no sand, it remained fierce. And now it was cold.

Her fists tightened around her camel rope as more rocks

clattered down into the gorge. Then suddenly her camel's hooves slipped on loose sand. The beast scrambled wildly, front legs buckling as it lost footing, and Nikki was tossed forward over the saddle. She screamed, grabbing wildly for the rope, but her camel got to its feet and scampered up the path. Nikki hit ground hard. She rolled twice like a rag doll. Then she began to slide toward the cliff edge.

She screamed again, digging nails into stone, trying desperately to find purchase, but couldn't hold…she was going over.

Dread slicked through her stomach as she felt herself dropping through the air. She bounced against a rock, grabbing wildly as she slid farther along the steep face. But all she succeeded in doing was releasing a shower of sand and stones that avalanched down with her. With a sharp jolt she hit a small ledge. Breath whooshed from her chest. She heard Zakir calling her name, but she couldn't breathe, couldn't call out to him. Rocks clattered down. One smacked her temple.

Blood leaked down the side of her face as nausea roiled in her gut. She wasn't sure if she could move her legs. She tried to turn her head, but as she did, the sandstone ledge she was resting on crumbled along the edges, more rocks clattering down into the abyss below her.

If she moved, the ledge would break.

Nikki inched her head again, this time to look down. As she did, dust dribbled out from the ledge, small stones clicking down, down, down.

Terrified, disoriented from the bash on her head, she lay dead still, blood trickling down her temple.

"Nikki!"

She didn't dare move again. "Down…here," she managed to rasp.

"Hold on! I'm coming to get you!"

No. He couldn't. It was a sheer drop of crumbling sandstone.

But he moved somewhere way up above her and a shower of sand and rocks cluttered down on her head. She tried to dodge sideways a little. More sandstone crumbled and sifted out from beneath her ledge. Her throat closed in on itself.

She couldn't look down. Too far. She closed her eyes. Shaking inside.

She hadn't felt such intense fear since that Christmas Eve when the black SUV had rammed into her, sending her spinning on ice, sliding through snow, crashing through the bridge barrier. She'd had the same gut-hollowing sensation the instant she'd realized her car was going over, plunging down, down, down to the highway below, her twins waking up in the back. The nauseating crunch of metal. The lights from the oncoming semi. Brakes. Swirling snowflakes. The truck sliding sideways, trying to stop, out of control on the ice.

Nikki scrunched her eyes tight, trying to block the sounds—the screeching, crunching, Chase's screaming. Silence from Hailey's crumpled, bloodied body.

She felt the cold in her bones as she remembered Chase in the emergency room as they tried in vain to pump life back into his little body. The unbearable grief of losing everything that was dear to her.

The shocking realization that the driver of the black SUV had been hired by her own husband to run her off the road.

She'd been planning to file for divorce, suing for custody of the children. She'd intended to expose Sam's affair. If she had, Sam would have lost access to Nikki's substantial inheritance. He'd have lost his kids. His reputation would have suffered.

So he'd tried to have her eliminated instead, she was sure of it. Yet she couldn't prove a thing.

She thought she'd seen a black SUV following her on several occasions. Once before it had tried to run her off the road when she was driving alone. She'd confronted Sam about it, and he'd laughed mockingly, said she'd imagined it. Then on Christmas Eve Nikki had gone to a colleague's party. She wasn't supposed to have the kids with her that night, but her sitter had called in sick at the last minute, so Nikki had taken the twins with her, just for a quick visit.

They'd been asleep when she'd left the house, and her friends had helped her carry them to her car, which had been parked in the garage. They'd been sleeping in the back when she'd backed out of the garage into the snowy driveway. Sam's hired gun had no way of knowing they were in the vehicle with her.

Sam had lost it when he learned he'd killed his children instead.

He tried to blame Nikki for their deaths. He leaked to the media that she'd been at a Christmas party that night and that she'd been driving drunk with her kids sleeping in the back.

The press jumped on it—big-shot senator's wife falls from grace. Top surgeon under investigation. And when the police found nothing—she'd only had one glass of wine—Sam slapped her with a massive civil suit instead.

Nikki simply lost the will to fight. Sam was just too damn shrewd and powerful, a narcissistic sociopath. He had all the contacts. People wanted to stay in his graces—he was being groomed for a run at party leadership. She'd tried everything to numb the grief, the gnawing sense of loss. Drugs. Alcohol.

She'd spiraled so badly, tried so hard to lose herself.

Nikki dug her nails into her ledge. She would *not* let herself fall. Never again.

She forced herself to remember the television ad for Mercy Missions that had saved her six years ago. And she remembered her orphans, waiting for her to return. Hot tears filled Nikki's scrunched-up eyes. She gritted her teeth against the sand in her mouth.

She had to try to get back up the cliff. For them.

Another shower of stones rained over her body. It was Zakir. Somehow he was coming closer.

She sucked air in deep, blinking blood from her eyes, and reached very carefully, slowly for the cliff wall. Terror rose in her throat again as more stones dislodged beneath her. But she found a hold, and inch by inch she pulled herself closer to the wall. Then she found another hold. She dug her fingers in. But the sudden shift in her weight broke the ledge, and with horror she felt it giving out under her. Slabs of sandstone thundered down into the gorge.

But just as she was about to go down, she felt his hand, solid, strong, clamping around her wrist. "Hold on, Nikki." His voice infused her with power, strength. She glanced up.

Relief gushed through her.

He had a rope.

He'd tied it to himself and was belaying down. "Grab my arm with your other hand and dig your feet into the cliff."

She sucked in her breath, counted to three and released her grip on the rock, slapping her hand over his arm. He braced. His rope stretched. She prayed it would hold them both. He held dead still for a moment, getting used to the additional weight.

"Okay," he said, breathless. "Good job, Nikki. Now I'm going to pull us both up. I want you to try and walk your feet against the wall. It'll take some pressure off. Just a few feet higher and the incline is much easier, okay?"

She nodded, more blood trickling into her eye.

And slowly, he began to work back up. It was hard, tedious work. Perspiration gleamed on his skin, and she felt the tremor of his muscles straining. More rocks skittered down from higher above. He ducked quickly, the motion knocking his glasses off his face. They clicked and clattered all the way down to the bottom.

He paused, catching his breath. Then slowly they began to move again.

Finally, they made it over the top, back onto the path.

They both just lay there for a moment, panting, trying to catch their breath, the realization of what almost happened suddenly becoming too raw, too real. Zakir's dogs milled excitedly around them, and Nikki saw with relief that the camels were still there.

He helped her to her feet. "Can you stand?"

"I…I think so. Just wobbly. Sore."

He guided her gently over to the leeward side of a rock outcrop. "Sit here. Did you break anything?"

"Just my head, I think." She smiled, suddenly insanely delirious with the idea she'd cheated death. Again. She was going to live.

And Zakir had saved her.

He grinned, pushing her matted and bloodied hair back to examine the gash on her temple.

"It's not deep, just messy." He retrieved a first-aid kit from the camel with the supplies, tore open a disinfectant wipe and began to clean the wound. It stung like hell and Nikki gasped, eyes watering. With another wipe he cleaned the side of her face, wiped the blood and sand from her eyes.

The tenderness in his powerful movements was suddenly overwhelming. To be touched, to feel protected, cared for, was something Nikki had not experienced in over seven years. She'd been walking such a solitary and secret road. And deep, deep down she'd felt so lonely, that to be touched like this made tears slide from her eyes.

He stilled as he saw them, then wiped them away, something shifting in him, too. "You're going to be fine, Nikki," he said gently.

She bit her lip and nodded. "Thank you. You saved my life, Zakir."

"How could I not?" he said quietly.

He was a different man out here, not afraid of being watched. Not afraid of touching. No need for political posturing. And she felt for him. He was in a tough position, and he was alone, like she was.

His dogs nudged him, impatient. It was getting dark, and the hounds sensed the coming night.

"We need to move, Nikki, find a place to set up camp before dark. It'll grow very cold, and there are jackals in these mountains. We can clean this wound better once we have cover."

He helped her to her feet and led her camel back to her. From the saddle pack she took another scarf, winding it over her head to protect her wound. Her nails were torn. She was covered in grazes, and she hurt all over. But she was still in one piece. Because of him.

Zakir began untying the rope he'd secured to a rock. The knots looked expert. Nothing had slipped. If they had, they both would have certainly tumbled to their deaths.

He'd risked his life to save hers.

"How'd you know how to do that?" she asked, nodding toward the rope. "Have you climbed?"

"Military training. And yes," he said, coiling the rope around his arm. "I've done a couple of expeditions, including an Everest summit." He smiled, and she was shocked by how gorgeous he looked when he did, a real warm genuine smile, white teeth against his dusky skin, rugged in this terrain. Natural. And without the dark glasses she could see the twinkle in his inky eyes.

"If you've got enough cash," he added with a laugh, "you can pretty much pay a team of experts to haul you up to the summit."

"Like you hauled me," she said, returning his smile.

He stilled for a moment, watching her, then he quickly

glanced away and got busy hooking the coil of rope back on the saddle pack.

"You lost your glasses," she said.

"Not a problem. My men can bring another pair." He didn't turn around, but she heard the shift in his tone. He didn't like the fact she'd noticed.

Once they'd secured their gear, they started to move again.

After twenty minutes, the path opened onto a dry moonscape surrounded by a cirque of ragged rocks. "We're on the right path," she called out with relief. "I recognize that circle of peaks. This is where the sentinels revealed themselves to me for the first time."

Zakir reined in his camel. He shielded his eyes, scanned the barren windswept terrain. "They'll be watching now," he said. "We can set up camp here. We'll be less of a threat if we show we have nothing to hide."

They dismounted, and together they began setting up the tent. Nikki took orders from him, working to secure ropes, her fingers sore, her head throbbing. Darkness was falling fast. Already he'd lit a fire for warmth and light. Zakir worked efficiently with his hands, and he seemed familiar with these simple tasks.

He caught her watching. "What is it?"

She shrugged, the movement painful, making her wince. "I did not expect this, you risking your life to come alone with me in the mountains."

He crooked up a dark brow, laughed low and guttural, and it stirred something in her belly. "Looks like you risked your own life back there, Nikki." His expression sobered. "It was a damn close shave," he said quietly. "Come sit here by the fire with me."

He draped a wool blanket over her shoulders as she sat. "Let's take another look at this gash."

She winced as he cleaned it out properly. "You could've just put me on a plane to the United States, you know, like you threatened. Why didn't you?"

He inhaled deeply, dabbed at her cut. It made her eyes water. "Because I really do need you to facilitate my meeting with the Berber sheik, Nikki. I've been focused exclusively on the seat of government in Al Na'Jar, at the expense of these no less important rural areas. You reminded me that these tribes could be a cornerstone in my success as a ruler. And I had to seize the opportunity when it arose. You gave me a way in."

This man was definitely not the tyrant she first thought.

"Besides, I've always taken risks—in business, pleasure. It puts you ahead of others who are afraid. It adds a bite to life." He smiled. His eyes liquid, beautiful, unguarded. "And I don't believe I'll come to harm in your presence. I'm no threat to them without my military convoy and Gurkhas."

She was quiet for a moment. "You really trust those Gurkhas."

"More so than I can anyone else. They have no allegiance to either side of the war here. They're completely neutral. Paid to do a job."

Guilt burrowed into Nikki. She should tell him, but she couldn't. She believed that Gelu would hurt her children.

He stirred the pot of soup he'd put over the fire. Silence fell over the camp, broken only by the crackle of flames and the sound of his hobbled camels pulling at dry tufts of scrub between rock cracks behind the tent. He'd fed his dogs, and they slept quietly, ears attuned to sounds.

He spooned soup into a mug and handed it to her.

"You're quite the renaissance man, Zakir," she said, taking the mug with both hands.

He glanced up. "Meaning?"

"Meaning you climb mountains, rescue women in distress, bandage them up, rule countries and corporate empires, ride camels, pitch tents." She sipped from her mug. "And you make very good soup."

He laughed. Yet the hint of respect in her eyes affected him. And with surprise Zakir realized he liked praise from Nikki. She was not one to waste words on triviality or flattery with ulterior motive. Not like the women he'd been wasting time with for the past decade of his life.

"You're not too shabby yourself, Nikki. We could make a good team."

The implications hung, silent, suddenly slightly uncomfortable.

"Tell me," he said, sipping his soup. "Why did you come to Africa? What made you pack it all up in America?"

She stiffened. "I came…because I needed to."

It was all she said. Curiosity rustled deeper in Zakir. "Did you leave family behind? A relationship?"

Her mouth tightened. She glanced at him, eyes narrowing. "No," she said. "I didn't leave a relationship. I… We'd separated before I came to Africa."

"An amicable separation?"

"What business is it of yours?" she snapped.

"Everything in Al Na'Jar is my business, Nikki."

"You mean an excuse to pry into personal lives."

"I wasn't prying. I'm interested."

She caught his gaze, and he saw a flash of pain. Then it was gone.

"I'm going to guess it wasn't a happy ending. Was it a marriage?"

She was silent for several long beats. "Yes, it was."

"But no children?"

She paused. "I've never had children."

She stood suddenly, holding the blanket tightly around her shoulders. She looked pale, drained. Firelight caught her hair, dancing gold on the curls. Even with matted sand and blood in her hair, she looked beautiful to him.

"I need to sleep."

He nodded. "Go ahead," he said gently. "I'll keep watch out here."

Zakir felt wide-awake, adrenaline pumping through his veins. He'd been energized by this day—and by Nikki's company. It was a long time since he'd felt this good, this vital.

As the flames crackled and shot orange sparks into the night sky, he wondered what kind of man would let a woman like Nikki go. And as he wondered what had happened to her relationship, Zakir realized that if she was hiding anything from him it was personal, and it had to do with her past. He felt it was unlikely she'd come to his country with intent to harm or spy on him.

Perhaps she was unable to have her own children. This could explain her obsession with her orphans.

Then again, he had yet to lay eyes on those orphans. Until he did, he couldn't fully trust her. And it was one of the reasons he wouldn't sleep tonight.

Instead, he sat by the fire, just sensing the desert, as he had as a boy.

He looked up at the stars. How much longer would he be able to see them? How many nights did he have until he went fully blind? Zakir was suddenly glad Nikki had arrived at his palace gates, because it had brought him here. She'd given him this one night, all alone under the Sahara sky. Just one more time.

The desert wind grew soft, and he heard an owl. He thought of his father, and how they'd all camped and hunted out in the Sahara—him, Tariq, Omair, Da'ud. Hot emotion filled his eyes. He missed them. He missed his mother. And as he looked up at the stars, Zakir vowed that their deaths would be avenged, that his enemies would take no more from him.

And nothing more from this land.

He got up, checked on Nikki, watching her sleep. Her hair shimmered around her face in the moonlight. He was glad, too, to be able to see her beauty. It was things like this that he would remember when darkness was complete. She stirred suddenly, her blanket slipping. Zakir could see the outline of her breast, rising and falling with each gentle breath. His groin stirred. He smiled ruefully and ducked back out of the tent.

Positioning himself on his stool, he threw another log on the fire.

This was not the time for romantic engagement. His duty was to his country, to fulfilling his father's will.

To making a marriage contract that would protect his power.

Chapter 8

Nikki awoke stiff and sore. Gingerly, she fingered the wound on her temple. The skin felt swollen, but not infected. She thought of how close she'd come to dying and was grateful again that Zakir had managed to save her life.

It had bought her another day to get her kids to safety. And excitement began to trill through her. If all went well, she'd see them today. She smoothed her hair, tied it back with a cord and put on a scarf. She rubbed her face, then bent to step out of the tent.

The dawn light was beautiful. The wind was still and temperatures had not yet started to climb. She saw Zakir near the path, already busy loading the camels. His dogs gamboled at his feet, frisky in the crisp air.

"Good morning," she called.

He stilled, staring at her as she neared. "Ready to leave?"

She nodded, suddenly uneasy. She hadn't meant to reveal so much of herself last night. Secrets were heavy, stressful things, and a part of Nikki craved the release of confiding in someone. But she couldn't.

Not if she wanted to keep her new life.

After taking the tent down and packing it onto the camels, they once again began to climb higher into the stark mountains.

As they crested a ridge, the sun burst over the peaks, rippling reds and yellows and golds into the dry hills. A hare bounded through scrub, and a vulture wheeled up high.

The warmth against Nikki's skin was instant, and she felt her camel's energy surge. So did hers when—as they rounded the next bend—the crumbling ruins of an ancient Crusades castle came into view. She relaxed. She was definitely on the right path.

But she gripped her camel rope suddenly, halting the animal when the first Rahm sentry stepped out into the track, brandishing an AK-47, his black robe and kaffiyeh flapping in the wind. Leather bandoliers crisscrossed his chest. His beard was long, ragged; his body wiry; and his skin darkly sun-browned.

Nikki carefully raised her arm high.

"I come in peace!" she called out in Arabic, her voice being snatched by wind and tossed through the scoured sandstone cliffs. "I return with a guide and medicine for my children. And with gifts of food and cloth from Sheik Zakir Al Arif!"

Silently, the sentinel motioned for her to dismount. She coaxed her camel into a couch. Zakir did the same, remaining behind her.

Dark shapes began materializing against the dun colored hills, black robes snapping in the wind.

More armed Berbers.

All wore the trademark leather cartridge belts crossed

over their chests. In her peripheral vision, Nikki saw more movement in rocks behind them. They were surrounded.

Nerves skittered. Her mouth turned dry.

Zakir drew up closer behind Nikki. He could feel her tension, and his hand shifted, ready to grasp the hilt of the scimitar hidden under his cloak.

The sentry motioned for Nikki to approach.

"Go," whispered Zakir. "I'm following right behind you. Tell them who I am right away, or they'll feel deceived." He noted the positions of the men in the hills as he and Nikki began to move slowly forward. They'd chosen a good place for an ambush. These mountain men were skilled guerrilla strategists who knew this harsh terrain like the backs of their hands. They were the kind of warriors Zakir could use on his side.

Not against him.

Which was why this meeting would be so important.

The sentinel lowered his weapon, eyes narrowing. Then suddenly his face crumpled into a craggy smile, teeth startling white against his dark features. "We have been waiting for your return, *malaak er-ruhmuh!*"

An angel, or messenger of mercy. These tribespeople regarded doctors and nurses as conduits of their God's mercy and healing power. They saw Nikki as a healer, thought Zakir.

"We are deeply pleasured to see that you have returned."

She bowed her head. "Thank you."

The men began to move closer, circling in behind them. Zakir's dogs began to bark.

He issued a curt order, and they stopped. But the men tensed, regarding him with fresh suspicion.

"Tell them," he whispered. *"Now."*

"I...I have much news," Nikki said quickly. "But first..." Her voice caught. "How are my children?"

"They wait for you, *malaak er-ruhmuh*."

Her body sagged, and her eyes filled with moisture. "All… of them?"

"All of them." Another smile, bright against his complexion. "Young Solomon told us you would return, that you would never desert them. He said you are their mother and guardian. Their angel."

A dry sob racked through Nikki's body. Zakir felt emotion swell in his own throat as he watched her. Her orphans were alive. They really did exist.

"Come!" The Berber held out his hand. "Welcome back to our home. What is this news you bring?"

Her gaze flicked around the sentinels. Zakir could see she was afraid. "I…I would like to introduce you to my guide. He, too, comes in peace." Her voice was thick and she spoke in careful Arabic. The men stilled, sensing something.

Zakir stepped forward, arms held slightly out to his sides so the warriors could see he had no weapon. He bowed slightly.

"I have come to meet your sheik," he said. "I have a great deal to learn from him and to share with him."

"Who are *you?*"

"I am Sheik Zakir Al Arif. I am your new king."

Tension rippled like some invisible crackling current among the men. Weapons turned on him and the silence grew dangerous.

Zakir couldn't help feeling admiration for these rebel warriors standing with unwavering stature, AK-47s aimed at his heart. There was a wildness about them, something primitive that spoke of desert history—that reminded Zakir of his ancestors in the paintings at his palace. It awakened something wild and abandoned in his own blood. He felt a whispering of heritage, a strange stirring of kinship.

"I come in peace," he reiterated, using the rough guttural

dialect of the mountains. "I have no soldiers, no guards with me. Will you take me to your sheik?"

The sentinel assessed him in silence.

"First you will give us the knives under your cloak."

Telegraphing each movement, Zakir slowly removed his scimitar belt, then his jambiya. He set them on the ground and then stepped back. One of the Berbers moved in to retrieve them while the others kept rifles trained on the Dark King.

"Bring the camels," said the sentinel with a jerk of his chin.

Zakir lowered his head, then led the camels forward, his dogs silent shadows at his heels.

Relief surged through Nikki. Zakir's humility had surprised her. Once again, his actions stirred her respect and admiration.

The convoy—tribesmen, camels, dogs, Zakir and Nikki—walked in silence through twisting sandstone cliffs and spires.

As they neared the hidden Berber village—many dwellings carved right into a massive cliff face, making the interiors cavelike and cool in the searing heat of summer, yet easily warmed by fire on freezing winter nights—a lone little figure bulleted down the path toward the procession on skinny little brown legs, one foot tripping over the other in his excitement. "Miss Nikki! Miss Nikki!"

"Solomon!" she cried.

"I told them you would come! Miss Nikki, I told them, and you are here!"

Choking on emotion, Nikki dropped down to her knees as Solomon—all of seven years old—barreled into her chest, skinny little arms wrapping like a limpet around her neck.

She hugged him tight, tears of relief streaming down her face as the Berber tribesmen and Zakir looked on. Then she held him out at arm's length so she could see his face, his glistening dark brown eyes, his bright white smile. "You were right, Solomon. How are the others? Did you take good care of everyone?"

He nodded again, pride squaring his skinny little shoulders and burning savagely into his dark eyes—wise, capable beyond his years. "I did my best, Miss Nikki, but they are very sick," he said in French.

"Samira?"

"She cannot walk, Miss Nikki. She is bleeding. The baby, it wants to come. Samira says so." Solomon's little hand sought hers, slipping into hers, fingers curling tight, and he tugged. "Come, come bring the medicine. Fix her."

Nikki felt Zakir's hand on her shoulder. She glanced up.

His black eyes had turned liquid, mysterious. "Go. I will talk with the Berber sheik."

She got to her feet, hesitated, recalling the words of Tenzing Gelu.

I want to know everything he says, who he meets with, each name.

Solomon tugged on her hand. The children were her priority. She was going to do whatever was necessary to keep them alive. "Help me with the medicine box, Solomon," she said, starting toward the camel with supplies.

"Nikki—" Zakir called after her suddenly.

She paused, heart skittering.

He came close, spoke low near her ear, in English. "I am pleased to see there are actual children. That your story is true."

She swallowed. He was finally beginning to trust her.

And now she would have to betray him.

Chapter 9

The afternoon light was low, the sun beginning to drop behind the hills. As Nikki bathed Samira's forehead she wondered what Zakir was doing, how his talks were going.

The image of Gelu's cold eyes snaked back into her mind, and she shivered slightly. How was she going to get out of this?

A shadow darkened the entrance of the small adobe hut. Nikki stilled, her hand resting on Samira's hot forehead. She sensed it was Zakir. Guilt reared up inside her, and her pulse began to race.

Slowly she glanced up.

He filled the doorway, a dark silhouette in a black tunic and riding boots, scimitar at his hip, the bejeweled hilt of the jambiya sheathed at his waist catching the fading light.

Her heart began to thud.

"It's okay," she whispered softly to Samira. "It's the king. He's here to help us."

Nikki bought a few moments to compose herself by

carefully squeezing out the cloth, saving the precious water droplets in a clay bowl. She stood, wiped her hands on her skirts and approached him. His stillness was unsettling.

He'd resumed his regal stance. Gone was the man she'd glimpsed alone in the mountains.

Zakir stepped back and out the door as Nikki came near, and she followed him into the sunlight. She looked up at his face and was startled by the intensity in his gaze. And again, studying him closely, she saw that the pupil in his left eye was not reacting to the rays of the sun setting behind the peaks.

"I wanted to thank you for being my envoy, Nikki. I misread you. The Berber shepherd has told me how you saved him and brought him back to the village."

Nikki heard admiration in his voice. Emotion punched so powerfully through her that she had to tighten her jaw, her fists, to hold it all in. "Thank you, Zakir," she whispered.

For respecting me. For admiring me.

She'd felt like a pariah for so long, been so filled with self-loathing over the way she'd handled her grief, that to earn this man's respect was almost overwhelming.

"You didn't expect this?"

She shook her head, laughed—an exhalation of relief. Then she inhaled shakily, pressing her hand against her sternum. "You keep surprising me. I guess I misjudged you, too."

"Is that young girl in the hut the one who is pregnant?"

Nikki nodded. "Samira."

"How is she?"

"Not good, I'm afraid. The baby is not due for another eight weeks, but Samira's been having contractions, bleeding. She's very dehydrated, and she has a fever. The baby is also in transverse lie—"

"Which means?"

"The fetus is lying sideways in the uterus. Sometimes you can get it to change position before labor starts by doing what is called an external version where you manually try and shift the baby."

"And if you can't?"

Nikki wiped her brow with the back of her sleeve, suddenly feeling exhausted. "Then it could become stuck during labor, and without surgical intervention the mother will die. If I can't turn the baby soon, Zakir, Samira will need to be in a hospital before she enters labor. And I'm worried about the contractions she is having now. Premature labor could be induced by a long journey to Tenerife. She really shouldn't travel." She sighed. "I'm not sure what to do."

Apart from performing an emergency C-section in primitive medical conditions. Nikki prayed it wouldn't come to that.

Zakir's eyes narrowed as he studied her, and something shifted in his dark, rugged features. Nikki thought again about how she'd felt under his body with his mouth a breath away from hers, the way she had stirred to life deep inside.

She flushed, swallowed. "I…I should get back to her."

He gave a curt nod, as if irritated with himself. Then he wavered, as if not wanting to let her go yet. "How are the other children?" he said, voice crisp.

"Much better. The hydrolytes helped with dehydration and the antibiotics with the stomach infections. They'll get strong again with…" Tears overwhelmed her as she spoke, and she angrily swiped them away with the base of her thumb. "Sorry. I'm tired, Zakir. I'm just so relieved to be with them again, to have brought them this far."

He placed his hand on her shoulder. Heavy. Warm. Such a calming strength transferring from his touch through her body. It was a gesture as potent as it was subtle, a message of affection, kinship, a sign that she should not feel so alone.

"And your wound—it's okay?"

She nodded. "I'm fine."

"Go," he said softly, rich, low. Authoritative. "Tend to your children. I will be meeting with the clan sheik and his tribal council later tonight. Other chiefs are coming from villages in the surrounding mountains. This has been made possible through your diplomacy, Nikki. I thank you for this. I will come and see the other children later—tonight." Almost reflexively, he gently, very briefly cupped the side of her face.

Heat rippled through Nikki, pooling low in her belly.

Then he was gone, striding away, his long gait eating up the distance to the main huts of the clan council.

She swallowed, composing herself before ducking back into the dark cool of the hut.

"Was that really the king?" Samira whispered in French.

"Yes, it was." Nikki placed the damp cloth on Samira's forehead, her heart squeezing at the smile crossing the child's thin face, the sudden glimmer of light in her huge dark eyes.

"We will be all right, then, Miss Nikki, with a king's help."

I hope so.

"Yes, we will—I know it in my heart, Samira," she lied. "And you must believe it, too. You and your baby will be just fine." As she spoke, memories of her own toddlers sifted into her mind. Pain stabbed through Nikki, her eyes growing moist again.

She clenched her teeth. Nikki needed to do this—she *had* to save Samira and her unborn baby. It might give some reason to why her own two precious little souls were stolen from her.

"He's very handsome," whispered Samira.

A breath of laughter burst through Nikki's tears, and she wiped her eyes. "You think so? How could you even see his face in this light?"

"I saw. I saw that he likes you."

Nikki stilled.

Her pulse quickened, along with something else, a little trill through her stomach. But she said nothing. Because she knew Samira was right—and it frightened her.

Later that night Nikki crept quietly up to a hut and pressed herself against the clay wall still warm from the sun. From this vantage point she could remain hidden while she tried to catch snatches of the tribal council debate around a fire that had been lit at the center of the village. The flames crackled, shooting hot orange sparks into the cool, dark sky.

Headmen from neighboring clans had traveled to join the Rahm sheik's council, and he and his men were passing a hookah around the fire as they listened to Zakir. The rich scent of tobacco reached Nikki as a young male attendant placed fresh charcoal in the clay water pipe.

The discourse was growing animated. Suddenly, Zakir leaned forward, his eyes locking with those of the clan sheik.

The men fell silent. Nikki tensed.

Even sitting on the ground, Zakir exuded a larger-than-life commanding presence. Tonight he wore his flowing black cloak against the mountain chill, and his hair fell loose and shiny to his shoulders. The flames caught the angles of his regal features, and his black eyes flashed as they reflected firelight—eyes that were failing him. Nikki's heart compressed involuntarily at the thought.

Blindness was going to be a real challenge for a man who liked to control everything.

Zakir broke the tension around the fire with an abrupt movement of his arm as he uttered something to the sheik, his voice resonating with the bass and guttural tones of the rough Rahm dialect. The sound rippled over Nikki's skin, warming her stomach. She could not take her eyes off him. She was mesmerized by this fireside vignette of what was possibly a historic political discussion.

The Berber sheik replied, his tone low, earnest, and the rest of the men leaned forward in interest. Zakir spoke again, saying something about representation at key government levels, and heads nodded in agreement. Nikki noticed that every now and then, almost as if subconsciously, Zakir's hand went to rest on the head of Ghorab who was lying with the two female salukis—Khaya and Tala—in the sand at his side. She leaned against the wall and just watched him for a while, enjoying the residual warmth from the clay spreading through her body.

Enjoying the look of him.

It was a guilty pleasure she hadn't allowed herself in years, just appraising a good-looking male. It also made her uncomfortable, reminding Nikki of who she used to be and of all the things she used to want—family, children of her own. The love of a good man.

But even as she was being inexorably pulled toward the king, attracted by his shimmering power and charisma, she feared his control over her emotions, her body. Because deep down, these were the same reasons she'd fallen for Sam.

Nikki had been a powerful and influential professional in her own right—an accomplished and feted surgeon who'd been drawn toward the intoxicating sensuality of a powerful, good-looking and sharply intelligent man. Sam had represented a challenge to her, and a promise of something incredible—in bed and in life. And look what had happened.

Sam had tired of her, started having affairs…

Against her will, memories whispered again, the desert night enveloping her with cold images of that tragic, snowy Christmas Eve. Nikki glanced up at the cliff silhouetted against the light of a pale moon. And she told herself she really had nothing to fear. Her children were healing, and

Zakir had infused her with hope that they'd all make it to the Canary Islands soon.

Once she was away from him she could forget her past self again. She could stop the ugly memories of Sam again, stop worrying about her fraudulent identity being exposed.

Nikki started as she felt a warm little hand slipping into hers. She glanced down and smiled as Solomon's eager eyes peered up at hers, glistening pools in the darkness. "Can you please sing us the bedtime story, Miss Nikki?"

She crouched down. "Of course, Solomon, I'll be right there. You go on ahead." She ruffled his head of tight dark curls. "Make sure the others are all lying down on their sleeping mats, okay?"

He ran off into the darkness. An owl hooted softly, and Nikki glanced once more at Zakir holding court. The king barked something angrily in Arabic, stabbing his jambiya forcibly into sand as he launched to his feet. She strained to hear, but the rough dialect eluded her. He stood, looming above the men, arms akimbo, his dark cloak lifting in the breeze, the bejeweled hilt of the scimitar at his hips catching firelight.

Dead silence descended over the men.

And then they suddenly broke out into knee-slapping laughter. Ghorab got up and yipped, followed by the excited barking of the two female salukis.

Relief rippled through Nikki.

For a moment she'd thought negotiations had turned sour. She had no idea what Zakir's joke was, but she found herself smiling as she turned and made her way to the orphan's hut. After all that the children had endured she was pleased to have been able to expose them to a community where jokes and laughter were a part of life, where the notions of family, respect and honor were sacrosanct.

Whatever diplomatic wizardry Sheik Zakir Al Arif was

busy weaving around those orange flames in the velvet desert night, Nikki knew instinctively it would be for the better—for both the Berber clans and Al Na'Jar.

Darkness was complete, the fire dying to red embers in the diplomatic circle. Above, in the inky vault of sky, stars were flung as if by supernatural hand. The wind had died, and all was still.

But tonight Zakir's sight was not good, and he could not visually appreciate the beauty of a Sahara night sky.

Anger stung him. He hated from the depths of his heart that he could not win the war against this one physical weakness in himself.

A soft and magical sound rose into the air, distracting Zakir from his emotions. Singing—a woman's voice, gentle, lyrical—came from the orphans' adobe hut, where a candle glowed through a narrow window. Zakir reached for Ghorab's collar and coaxed his dogs toward the blurry gold flickering in the dark.

As he neared, he realized with a surprising surge of pleasure that the voice was Nikki's and that she was singing a story in French.

Zakir walked quietly toward the hut, not wanting to make any sound that might telegraph his presence, simply hungry to listen to her voice. A jackal yipped somewhere in the hills as it hunted, and Zakir abruptly silenced his dogs, signaling them to lie at his boots. He leaned his shoulder against the mud wall and listened for a while, his pleasure deepening as he realized that he recognized the words of her story.

It was an ancient desert fable from his own youth, one his mother, Nahla, used to sing to Zakir and his siblings. His mother had told them the story had been passed down from nomadic Bedouins who used to sing it to their children while they traveled from the Western Sahara all the way to the Caspian Sea.

Bewitched by the threads of story and song, the king was inexorably pulled back to memories of the boy he once was.

The exact words of the tale varied across the Sahara, but essentially the story was the same—about a princess stolen by warriors and sold into slavery. She was bought at a North African market by emissaries of a strange and mysterious man who some said was a chimera who shifted between king and animal.

The princess was taken to this man's desert castle, and while she never actually got to see him since he moved about his palace only by night, she was taught by staff to fear him. The orphan princess was also taught the dance of the veils.

"And then—" Nikki's voice switched from song into a soft whisper "—when she was old enough, one night the princess was summoned to dance before this mysterious king. And she danced and danced, swirling in her veils, and then the king said to the slave girl, 'Now you must sing for me.' And the slave girl did." Nikki's own voice rose in song, and Zakir felt in himself a rush of anticipation and warmth as he recalled his mother's voice singing these same words in Arabic while he, Da'ud, Tariq and Omair sat listening rapt at her feet, and tiny Dalilah, who was just an infant at the time, slept in his mother's arms.

Transported, Zakir inhaled deeply and closed his eyes, allowing his other senses to absorb this moment. Nikki's voice wrapped around him like soft velvet, bringing even more memories of family, comfort, a time when everything was right in his young world.

And in his heart Zakir suddenly yearned to return to that place of family and togetherness. He longed to feel inside himself the pure love that he'd glimpsed in his father's eyes as the then king had looked upon his mother.

Nikki reached a verse where the children's voices joined hers, a little orphan choir rising in song, high in the barren hills of a desert night—children of violence, singing with such innocence and purity and beauty that it could make a man weep.

This surely was the essence of life, of the future. Especially for a country like his. And Zakir realized suddenly that this childlike purity that could still be coaxed from these abused war orphans was the very thing that Nikki sought so desperately to save.

Compelled, hungry for something he could not even begin to articulate, Zakir reached forward and carefully edged aside the curtain that hung over the door. He peered inside, eyes trying to adjust to candlelight.

Nikki's face was turned away from him. He could see the blur of her profile, skin like porcelain. She wore no scarf, and her golden hair fell across her face in a cascade of loose curls. She looked like an angel.

Around her feet, on seven reed mats on the dirt floor, were the children. Each pair of dark eyes was turned toward Nikki, their voices earnest as they sang the fairy-tale words of Zakir's youth.

The eldest child, Samira, caught his movement at the door. She glanced up and abruptly stopped singing. Like an electric current rippling through the other kids, they all fell instantly silent and spun to face him.

Zakir sensed their fear.

He cleared his throat, stepped inside the room. "I apologize," he said in Arabic, then French. *"Je suis desolé.* I wanted to listen, but not to disturb."

Nikki lurched to her feet, hand shooting to chest in surprise. "Zakir!" She hurriedly groped for her scarf to cover her hair. But he stepped forward and stayed her with his hand on her arm. "Please, don't."

She hesitated.

"I don't want you to hide yourself from me anymore," he whispered against her ear. Then loudly he said, "I just wanted to hear the story." He smiled and turned to the orphans, holding his hands out at his sides, palms up. "So, you must be the famous children who crossed the burning sands of the Sahara!"

A little boy bobbed his head and excitedly got up on to spindly brown legs. He bowed deep. "I am Solomon, your Royal Highness."

Zakir laughed with deep pleasure, and he crouched down, balancing on the balls of his feet as he peered into the young boy's dark eyes. "I know. And I am Sheik Zakir Al Arif, the King of Al Na'Jar. Can you introduce me to everyone else, Solomon?"

Pride swelled the little boy's chest.

Nikki's eyes glistened as she watched him, and for some damned reason Zakir wanted to do her proud, to not disappoint her. He wanted to see that glow of admiration in her eyes again. He wanted to ease the tension that seemed to permanently knot her shoulders.

"This is Philippe, Mahmoud, Lorita, Koffi and this is Lina—" Dusky faces broke into smiles as the children launched to their feet in turn and bowed in front of Zakir.

"And this is Samira," declared Solomon. "She's going to have a baby!"

Zakir's heart torqued with sudden ferocity as Samira, a mere child herself, lowered her dark head in reverence, her silken hair spilling forward. She had Arabic blood, like him, but with much browner skin—a child of mixed race and culture, born of violence, and carrying another conceived in violence. A cycle that never ended.

A cycle Nikki was fighting to stop.

Zakir shot a fierce a glance at Nikki, suddenly understanding the steel he'd glimpsed in her eyes. He now knew how she'd managed to walk up that deserted boulevard toward his tanks and guns. He understood the way in which she'd confronted him in his reception room.

He exhaled slowly, a little overwhelmed with the sudden rawness of affection he felt for her, and he turned to her children. "Did you all have enough dinner tonight?"

They nodded quietly.

Nikki picked up the candle, cupping her hand around the flickering light as she moved toward the door. "Time for sleep, *mes enfants*," she said fondly. "I will be back soon. I'm just going outside to talk with the king."

She carried the candle to the door and blew it out before exiting. In the sudden darkness, Zakir had to reach for the wall. He felt his way to the entrance and held back the reed mat for Nikki.

He knew she was watching.

They stepped outside, and Zakir clicked his fingers softly, his hounds surging to his side. He hooked his fingers into Ghorab's collar as they walked into the night. "How are they doing, Nikki?"

"Better."

"Samira? Have you been able to turn her baby?"

"No. And she's still running a fever."

He nodded quietly, leading her toward the dying fire with no real purpose other than talking to her out of earshot.

"Where did you learn that song, Nikki?"

"Do you know it?"

"My mother used to sing those words to us in Arabic when I was a child."

She stilled, looked up at him and smiled. Moonlight caught the slight gleam on her teeth and the shimmer of her eyes. It was all Zakir could see. But her smile did crazy things to his chest. Giving Nikki pleasure expanded Zakir in a way he could not define.

"Why are you smiling, Nikki?"

"Some men," she said quietly, "you just can't imagine as having been children."

He laughed. "Solomon will be like that someday. Mark my words. Overnight you will suddenly see only a powerful man, and you will no longer see the boy."

"And how would you know?" He heard the slight jest in her tone, a playfulness he had not detected before.

"I just do."

"Because you were like him?"

He shrugged, slipping effortlessly into easy conversation with her as they resumed walking, his dogs moving like shadows at their side. "I think Tariq was more like Solomon. Very earnest, helpful. He wanted to solve the world's problems. I was perhaps more quiet than Tariq. My mother used to call me broody, but I was not as sullen as Omair." He laughed again. "These Rahm Berbers might call me the Dark One, but Omair is the true dark horse. He's the one whose thoughts will never be read."

"Well, unless Solomon gets a break, he'll become like his father."

"And who was Solomon's father?"

"A warlord. Very cruel, very powerful. Solomon ran away."

"Why?"

"He was abused."

"He was lucky," said Zakir softly.

"How so?"

"Because he found you." Zakir paused, turned to glance down at her.

Moonlight caught the glisten of emotion in her eyes, but

she said nothing. And Zakir couldn't stop himself. He touched her cheek, in the dark, with no one to watch.

"Nikki," he whispered, her skin soft under his palm, cool in the night air. He moved his thumb under her chin, his fingers cupping the side of her face. "You are the most beautiful woman I have ever met." He brought his lips close to hers. "And I speak of much more than physical perfection," he whispered in Arabic.

A shiver trilled down Nikki's spine.

She swallowed, unable to speak, and she was suddenly, utterly desperate to lean into this man's hard, warm body, to feel his strength, to absorb more of the calm power he seemed to infuse with his touch.

It was such a human need—to be touched. Comforted. Loved. A need Nikki had tried to ignore for so long. And Zakir was forcing those long-buried desires to rise to the surface, making her burn with hunger for him.

He removed his hand abruptly, and she felt as if she'd been dropped from a safety net. Nikki cleared her throat, anxiety tearing through her desire. This man was too strong, too masculine, too sensual, and when she was around him her mind narrowed. It was as if she had no control.

And with her mounting panic, the stark reality of her situation returned. She'd been told to spy on Zakir—if she didn't, her children could be hurt. She was going to have to face that Gurkha. She *had* to give him something, and right now she had nothing.

"How did the meeting with the elders go?" Her voice came out husky as she changed the topic.

She felt his body go still, as if he was surprised by the question. An energy, soft and dark, crackled between them. Nikki's pulse began to race.

"The talks went exceedingly well," he said finally. "I learned from the Rahm sheik that my father often met with clans. The men knew my father as a person who loved the desert and its people, and so remained loyal to him. My father had also informed them about his plan for democracy. They were happy to learn that I will pursue this agenda, that they will one day have a voice in the government of Al Na'Jar." He paused. "Thank you again for your help, Nikki. It was good that I came without my guards."

"What did the chiefs from the surrounding villages say?"

"They're on board. Their support will enable a grassroots alliance along this entire eastern border region. If I can continue to foster relations like this among other Al Na'Jar clans, I can build support for my monarchy from the bottom up, and the handful of enemies inside my administration will be unable to topple me. Besides," he said, smiling, "it has been good for me to reconnect with these people. They are the essence of Al Na'Jar. They share my values."

"*Your* values?"

He laughed low, seductive. "Yes, Nikki. Values I'd forgotten in those boardrooms of Europe and in those nightclubs…" His voice grew distant as he glanced up at the sky. "In some ways it took this terrible family tragedy to bring me home."

Or perhaps it's your fear of impending blindness. The realization of your own vulnerability has shown you what really matters.

He took her arm. "This is unorthodox," he said very quietly, close to her ear, his breath sending a warm shiver over her skin. "But would you care to join me in my hut for a drink? It will be our last time alone before my Gurkhas arrive tomorrow."

"They're coming *here?*"

"The Berbers say my bodyguards are now welcome in the village. I sent for just three of them—Tenzing Gelu, Abhi Hasan and Rajah Sadal. They're en route by camel as we speak. The other two men have more experience in strategic planning, so they'll return to the Supreme Palace and select a bigger security team for me. I plan to spend some time building more alliances to the northeast and will be using the Summer Palace as a base for a while." He touched her elbow gently as he spoke, guiding her. "So, how about the drink, Nikki?"

Her heart thudded, perspiration breaking out over her skin. Everything was happening too fast. Gelu was already on his way. She needed to work out a plan.

"I'm exhausted, Zakir. But thank you for the invitation. For everything. You've given my children another window of hope."

And you've given me some self-esteem back.

Zakir nodded, disappointed and a little vulnerable for having vocalized his need and being rejected. In silence he led her back to her hut, using Ghorab, Khaya and Tala as guides.

She stopped outside the door. The scent of the desert was cool, tinged with residual smoke from the fire.

"Good night, Zakir." She began to pull the curtain back, but froze as he placed his hand on her shoulder.

"Nikki?" he whispered.

She straightened up slowly, and Zakir felt her lean toward him, as if wishing to linger with him. Then quickly resisting the urge, she reached again for the reed curtain. He caught her arm and turned her to face him.

Silence and tension simmered between them.

Shaded from the other huts, Zakir was unable to stop what came next. He threaded his hand into her hair and cupped the back of her neck. Lowering his head, drawing her into him, he kissed her lightly on the mouth. He felt her lips, soft, warm, open under his, and his vision spiraled into a red-and-black kaleidoscope of shadows as heat speared into his groin.

Her body seemed to sigh into his, as if every molecule in

her being wanted to give into her need for him, but it was only for a nanosecond. Because Nikki stiffened suddenly and drew back. Her eyes were wide and glittering in the dark, moonlit pools in a pale face. She stared at him, then ducked quickly into the dark hut.

As the reed curtain rustled back into place, Zakir felt hot, his mouth dry.

What in hell are you doing here?

Inhaling sharply, he turned, giving a soft whistle to his dogs. He hooked his fingers lightly around Ghorab's collar and made his way back to his hut where he paced the packed mud floor of the small interior, cursing himself.

Zakir believed he could trust Nikki enough to let her leave the country now. The presence of her orphans and the Berbers themselves had confirmed her story. She was a genuine and compassionate healer. She was not here to harm him—Zakir believed that.

So why was he messing with her, touching her? Why was he letting himself be distracted? He had a duty to fulfill, problems that needed attention. Like the insurgency. Like his rapidly failing vision. Like finding a wife.

Irritable, Zakir grabbed his satellite phone, dialed Tariq on the encrypted system.

This was his first moment of total privacy in a day, and he needed medical advice from his brother. He glanced at his watch as the phone rang. It would be late in Washington, but he knew Tariq, the dedicated neurosurgeon, would still be at his office. Zakir paced as he listened to the phone ringing an ocean and continent away, and his thoughts drifted back to Nikki and her haunting eyes. *Oyoon el waha,* he thought—eyes of the oasis. A place of sanctuary, in which a man could drown himself.

So absorbed was Zakir that he started at the sudden sound of Tariq's voice.

"Zakir?" His brother sounded concerned. "What is wrong? Has something happened?" he said in Arabic.

Zakir explained the sudden episodes of blurred vision and blindness. Tariq asked several questions, then fell silent for a moment. When he spoke again, Zakir's heart sank at his brother's tone.

"Once there have been several episodes of this nature and duration," said Tariq, "things could happen fast. Much faster than we at first anticipated. You will find vision in your left eye will go completely, first. This will be followed by decreasing central vision in the right eye, and then the optic nerves will fail completely in that one, as well."

"How fast?" Zakir said very quietly.

Tariq cleared his throat, "Perhaps within a few months the blindness will be permanent in both eyes."

Zakir clenched the phone. "A few months?" he whispered.

"It could even be weeks, or days." His brother was silent for a beat. "I am sorry, Zakir. You will need to marry soon, brother."

Zakir inhaled deeply, fist tensing around the phone. "I'll call my emissary in Europe right away, make it clear that I need to marry before the month is out."

"In the meantime, you can perhaps delay onset of blindness by taking medication to reduce blood pressure. You need to stay calm, Zakir. Stress will hasten vision loss."

Zakir laughed drily. Calm was not possible—not with the tasks that awaited him. But Tariq was right—the only way to safeguard the throne was to find himself a queen and to be officially crowned. Then he would quickly change the constitution so he could govern blind.

Al Arif Corporation lawyers in Paris had already drafted the contract that Zakir and his potential bride would sign. The candidate of his choosing would agree to a finite term, along with hefty financial compensation, during which she would appear on Zakir's arm as his queen. She would also try to bear him a child. After the term was up, and once Zakir's rule was secure, the marriage would be annulled by royal decree, unless both parties mutually agreed to extend the terms and remain married for an additional period of time.

"Shokrun ya akhi," he said crisply. Thank you, my brother.

He killed the call and sat on his bed, feeling the weight of the future on his shoulders. And suddenly Zakir wanted nothing to do with the women of his past—the kind who'd eagerly agree to marry and sleep with him for hefty monetary gain. The ones for whom he'd never hold any real affection.

He wanted Nikki.

Which was ludicrous. She was not the type to enter into a marriage arrangement for money. Besides, he barely knew anything about her. She'd have to be properly vetted. He'd have to hire an investigator to comb through her past in America.

Zakir lay back on his bed, hooking one arm behind his head while he kept the other on the hilt of his weapon. He would not sleep. Not until his bodyguards arrived. But as he lay there, the idea of possibly entering into a business arrangement with Nikki began to entice him on more levels than Zakir cared to admit.

Irrespective of his growing attraction to her, Nikki *was* potentially an ideal candidate. She spoke the language of his people, she loved his desert, she was bold and she seemed to be skilled at diplomacy. And as much as Zakir hated to think about it, he knew Nikki would be able to handle his blindness. He'd witnessed her capacity for tenderness in the way she cared for the children.

Malaak er-ruhmuh.

That's what the Rahm Berbers had called her. An angel.

It irritated him that he even wanted this kind of tenderness from a woman. Then he thought of the sensation of her mouth, soft and warm under his, and desire stirred in his groin.

Would she even think of doing it? Could he persuade her to enter into an official engagement with him while he secretly had her investigated?

Anticipation sparked through his chest—the old thrill of the hunt. And the more Zakir thought about it, the more sense it made. If she agreed, then he could immediately put her name before the King's Council as his potential wife. It would be a solid first step to securing his reign. It would send the right message to his enemies. Meanwhile, he'd continue to run his search for a wife in Europe. If Nikki's background check fell through for some reason, he'd still have an acceptable backup waiting in the wings, ready and vetted. And in the interim he'd have enjoyed the security—and the intimacy—of a betrothal.

I can get to know her better. I can touch her. Taste her.

But the clock was ticking. Could he do it? Could he manipulate Nikki into a betrothal of convenience—and seduce her into his bed—before he went blind?

Chapter 10

Dawn was harsh, the sky clear as Nikki went to the well for yet another pitcher of water. Samira had taken a bad turn during the night and was running a higher fever. Nikki was doing her best to keep her cool and hydrated.

But as she reached for the pump handle, she glanced up, saw two of Zakir's red-turbaned guards rounding the corner, kukri knives bumping against their thighs as they strode quickly toward the king's hut.

Fear shot up her spine. Quickly, she filled the clay pitcher and hurried back to the hut. She *had* to get Samira and the others out of here. She had to get away from Zakir and his men, this country. It was not her battle.

She elbowed the reed curtain aside, ducked into the hut and gasped, almost dropping the pitcher.

Tenzing Gelu.

Sitting on the edge of Samira's bed.

Nikki began to shake. "What are you doing in here?"

He stood, his mouth twisting into a crooked smile, his eyes

inscrutable behind mirrored shades. "I am merely checking that the village remains secure for the king."

"There's nothing in here. Get out, now!"

Samira's eyes widened into round, dark circles at Nikki's tone. The other children stilled, picking up on her fear.

Gelu placed one hand on the hilt of his knife and held the other out toward the door. "After you, Ms. Hunt."

She swallowed, her gaze flicking around the room. "Solomon, come, take this jug. Use the water to keep damp cloths on Samira's forehead."

"Where are you going, Miss Nikki?" Solomon watched Gelu as he spoke, his little fists balled tightly at his sides.

"I'm just going outside for a minute."

Worry etched into the small boy's features. "I'll be fine, Solomon. Here, take the jug."

"Yes, Miss Nikki." He solemnly took the water pitcher from her.

Nikki stepped out into the blazing sun, heart hammering. Gelu followed, motioning with a quick flick of his head for her to step behind the wall. He stood in front of her, one hand against the wall above her shoulder, his other resting threateningly on the hilt of his weapon. "What have you got for me, Ms. Hunt?"

"Don't you *ever* come near those children again," she growled at him.

He bent his head lower toward hers, dropping his voice. "If you cooperate, there will be no need."

Her gaze flicked around, desperate. But Gelu had chosen a spot where no one could see them. "I...I won't do this," she hissed. "I will *not* spy on Sheik Zakir."

"Then little Samira—" He smiled slowly at her surprise. "Yes, she told me her name. A very sweet girl. But she'll be dead by nightfall." His voice was cool. It held no intonation, no emotion. It made his threat all the more deadly.

Nikki felt blood drain from her face. She'd met men like him—the rebels in Mauritania. Sam. You didn't mess with a man like Gelu.

She had to buy time.

She had to give him something, anything. Preferably information he'd easily learn himself anyway. Information that would not hurt Zakir. "Sheik Zakir met with the chief of the Berber village and his council last night," she said quietly.

"What did they discuss?" Still no intonation.

A pearl of sweat slid down from her temple. "The Berbers will support him. There were other leaders from surrounding mountain villages there, too. Sheik Zakir will have their support as well."

"What else?"

"That's…all. I…I didn't understand the dialect very well."

He studied her for several long beats. "You need to do better than this."

She swallowed the ball of dry fear swelling in her throat. "He… The Berbers said they were pleased to hear that Sheik Zakir would be following in his father's footsteps and that he would begin a transition to democracy." She inhaled shakily. "The tribesmen are very keen to have representation at the government level."

Something darkened in him.

"You will continue to inform me as long as you remain close to the king. That is, if you truly wish to keep your children safe." Gelu swiveled abruptly and ducked around the side of the wall.

Nikki stood there, shaking.

She had to get out of this country. But she couldn't risk moving Samira now. She needed a plan. Wiping sweat from her brow, Nikki decided she would continue to feed Gelu superficial information about Zakir until Samira was safe to travel.

She had no other choice.

And once she was out of Al Na'Jar, she'd find a way to let Zakir know that he had a traitor in his midst.

Zakir strode with renewed vigor toward Nikki's hut. He was going to propose a betrothal arrangement, and defeat was not in his lexicon.

But as he neared he saw Nikki carrying a clay urn from the pump at the well. A determined urgency bit into her stride, her skirt swishing across her sandaled feet.

"Nikki!"

She swung around, eyes flashing. Disquiet furrowed into Zakir as he caught her expression. He clicked his fingers, distracting his hounds from sniffing something at a hut. "Is everything all right?"

She inhaled deeply. "It's Samira. The other children are fine to travel today, and I wanted to leave right away, but…" She looked crestfallen, broken suddenly in spirit. "Samira's fever is much higher, and because of it her cramps are increasing. She could go into labor soon, Zakir, and I haven't been able to turn the baby. She needs a hospital."

Energy coursed through him at this news. He placed his hand on her shoulder, hating himself for being thrilled at the excellent opportunity this afforded him. He knew Nikki cared more about her orphans than herself. They were a tool he could use to manipulate her into a betrothal.

"Nikki…" He infused his voice with the kind of calm authority he employed to sway high-powered but jittery investors around a boardroom table. "The hospitals in my country are in terrible shape at the moment—short on staff, devoid of equipment. I have a far, far better alternative for Samira and the other children. And for you."

And me.

"As I mentioned, I have further negotiations planned for the tribes to the north, closer to the Moroccan border," he said. "In order to make this easier, I will be staying at the Summer Palace in the north mountains. It is an ideal base for this operation. A fortress, well guarded, and the castle also has every facility, including a physician's surgery room. Bring your children there, and I will fly in the doctors and equipment you need."

"It's not possible, Zakir. Samira won't make a trip down the mountain on camel. I cannot move her."

"One of my Black Hawks will be landing here within the next hour. I summoned it earlier today. We can fly her at once. In fact, I will call Tariq right now and ask him to recommend and send a top obstetrician from the States."

Her lids flickered fast, her cheeks heating. She glanced quickly to the hills, as if suddenly seeking escape.

Frowning at her reaction to Tariq's name, Zakir continued. "You and your children can rest at the palace, Nikki, with the best care. Under my guard, your orphans will have an opportunity to just be children for a while, as you said you wished they could be. You can travel again once Samira's baby is born, once you are all ready."

Tears brimmed in her eyes, surprising him.

She remained silent for a long while, and he realized that her hands, still holding the heavy jug of water, were trembling.

"Forgive me," he said, reaching to take the clay pitcher from her. She angrily swiped her eyes with the back of her sleeve, struggling with something.

"Nikki?"

She inhaled deeply, looked away again. Then suddenly she steeled herself, and her eyes met his. "Thank you, Zakir. We will all be deeply grateful for your hospitality." She reached to take the jug of precious water back from him.

But something had shuttered in her, closing him off in some subliminal way.

Zakir was disturbed by how viscerally her rejection—even as she accepted his invitation—affected him.

No woman ever shunned him. This was a gauntlet thrown down, a challenge, and it stirred the hunter in him. It also sparked something else, a reminder to be careful. He still knew very little about her.

"There is one condition, Nikki," he said quietly.

Her shoulders flexed. "What?"

"It's a minor thing, a mere matter of appearances, but it could have severe consequences for my monarchy and my people. If you do choose to come to the Al Na'Jar Summer Palace, you must do so under the pretext that we are officially betrothed."

"Excuse me?"

"My country has laws, Nikki. I can change them by unilateral decree after my official coronation. But until then, I myself must adhere to them. One of those laws states that if an unmarried regent wishes to openly consort with a woman she *must* be betrothed to him, and her name must be officially put before the King's Council in this capacity so that they can vet her."

Her brow lowered. "So…you're technically a regent?"

"For want of a better term. Under Al Na'Jar law I am not the supreme monarch until I take an official oath and am officially crowned."

"Why haven't you taken this oath already?"

"You've seen the mess my country is in, Nikki. I simply haven't had the time." He omitted the part about first needing to find a wife.

"What exactly would the council vet me for?"

He pursed his lips, shrugged nonchalantly. "Technically

the council will want to be sure you are suited for the role of queen."

Her jaw dropped. *"Queen?"*

He raised his hand, halting her thought. "It's merely protocol, Nikki. A formality so that you can accompany me in public and in private. That is all."

She stared at him, clearly confused.

Solomon called from the door of the hut, "Miss Nikki, come!"

Attention suddenly rent in two, she shot a glance at the hut. "I... Samira needs me."

"Miss Nikki!"

"Can you accept this?"

She looked horrified. *"No.* I can't accept this."

He leaned closer, lowering his voice to a whisper. "You either accept this deal, Nikki, or I can no longer help you."

"Miss Nikki! Come quick!"

"I...I have to go." She spun around, spilling precious water from the urn as she hurried into the hut.

"I leave within two hours!" he called after her. "I'll need your decision by then."

Zakir realized his heart was hammering, his palms damp. Frustrated, he spun around and marched toward the Gurkhas waiting near his hut. "Prepare to leave for the Summer Palace," he barked. "The chopper will be here soon. And bring me my laptop," Zakir commanded as he ducked into his hut. One of his guards came running with a military computer equipped with satellite communication. At a folding table, Zakir began to draft strategy for his meetings with more rural clan leaders. He kept one eye on the time, growing increasingly edgy as he waited for Nikki's word.

Within an hour Gelu appeared at his door, indicating Nikki had come to see him.

Zakir nodded, returning his attention to his work as she

quietly entered his temporary dwelling. His plan was to play cool now, to wait and see where she placed her chess piece.

"We're ready to go with you," she said.

He glanced up, and compassion knifed him. Her face was pale, tight. Her gaze kept flicking nervously to his guards. Something had definitely switched in her—as if her road to freedom had suddenly been cut, and with it some spirit. Why would she feel this way when she should be grateful for his help?

"I am pleased to hear it," he said, rising to his feet.

She remained stiff near the hut door. "We should move Samira as soon as possible," she added.

He flicked out his wrist, checked his watch. "The helicopter should be here any minute now. So you are comfortable with my condition?"

"No, I'm not," she said. "But I'll do what I have to. For the children." But she wavered. "How will the council's vetting process be any different from the background check you've already run on me? Wasn't that enough?"

"It's essentially the same. Really, Nikki, this is just a formality." He paused, a little icicle of unease forming in his gut. "Is there something you want to tell me?"

Her gaze sliced into his. Aquamarine. Direct. "Of course not," she said, voice clipped. And she stepped out into the searing midmorning sun.

Zakir watched the reed curtain fall into place behind her, the icicle in his gut chilling his pleasure at winning the first move.

Maybe he hadn't won at all.

He thought again of how she'd just appeared at his palace and how quickly she'd worked her way into his life.

Maybe he was inviting an enemy right into his home—and

potentially into his bed. He didn't think so. In his heart, he felt she was true.

But would he be able to withstand the consequences if he was wrong?

Chapter 11

The Black Hawk thudded higher into the thin air over the northern mountain range, and as they drew closer to the Moroccan border Nikki grew increasingly tense over what she'd committed to. Her avenues to freedom seemed to be rapidly shrinking.

She told herself this was temporary. And it was best for Samira, who now slept soundly on the seat behind her and Zakir. Once Samira had had her baby, Nikki could leave with her children.

In the front seat of the modified cabin, Tenzing Gelu and Abhi Hasan sat facing them, ramrod straight, their eyes hidden behind reflective shades. Rajah Sadal sat at the rear of the chopper.

Far below, the desert terrain grew more lush the farther north they traveled. Peering out of the window, Nikki began to see wadis surrounded by thick groves of date palms. Olive orchards covered the ocher hills, and cerise bougainvillea clambered up the clay walls of Berber villages. A shepherd chased goats with a stick, his dusty robe flapping as he ran on sandaled feet.

The chopper flew above a dust road that wound into high peaks. Then, as they crested a rugged ridge, a vast plateau unfolded in front of them. The change in topography was so startling and so stunning that Nikki caught her breath. The area appeared blessed with a microclimate of its own—soft gold grasses blew gently in the wind along the rolling plains and juniper scrub dotted the far hills.

Suddenly, Nikki caught sight of the Summer Palace.

The walled compound was massive, with domes of gold that glittered in the sun and minarets that stabbed high into the clear, blue sky. The entire complex was cradled at the center of the vast plateau and had been built from rock with the same soft pink and ocher tones as the surrounding peaks. Towering palm trees lined the miles of road from the gateway to the castle where a riotous color of flowers erupted around shimmering rectangular pools.

Nikki saw why this region had been chosen for the location of a Summer Palace. Geographically, it was indeed a fortress as Zakir had said, accessed by only one very long and narrow twisting road in. And out.

"It's beautiful, Zakir," she whispered, overcome with awe. As she spoke, she heard the thud of more helicopters. Four Black Hawks appeared over the opposite ridge. They began to lower into the compound, palm leaves twisting violently in the downdraft.

"That's my security detail," Zakir said as he watched the helos landing. "Our pilot will set us down on the private landing pad at the south end of the palace."

She nodded, the sense of entrapment winding tighter and tighter the closer they got to the gleaming citadel. Their chopper began to descend into the compound.

"Those two men I sent to Al Na'Jar," he said, watching her

closely, as if sensing her mounting unease, "have also informed the King's Council and the court of our new status."

Nikki couldn't breathe for a moment. This meant they would have commenced another background check on her.

Would her identity continue to hold? Would Sam somehow be alerted in the process?

She literally felt her time running out. Clearing her throat, Nikki forced her voice to remain level. "How long will this vetting process take?"

He studied her in silence as the pilot lightly set his bird on the ground, and she felt her face growing hot. "You are very interested in this vetting process, Nikki."

"Of course I am," she whispered angrily as the rotors slowed, worried about how freely he spoke in front of his Gurkhas. Zakir had no idea what he could be exposing himself to with Gelu sitting there. And she didn't know if—or how many of—the others were also involved in his treachery. "I'm being forced to pretend I want to become queen of Al Na'Jar," she hissed. "I need to understand *exactly* what I've committed to."

His beautiful lips curved seductively, and she hated what his smile could do to her insides. She also hated the fact she couldn't read his eyes behind his new set of dark glasses.

"You are not bound by anything, Nikki," he said softly into her ear, his voice very low, French-Arabic accent rolling like warm water over her skin. "This is your choice. I will never force you to do anything you don't want to. Whenever you are uncomfortable, just tell me to stop."

She blushed. His words held promise of sex. It reminded her of the sensation of his lips against hers and how her body had reacted against her will.

"But you must tell me if you are hiding something about your past, Nikki. My enemies will be looking for *anything* they can use to undermine me and mount an official challenge to my rule." He smiled, but the expression held more threat than kindness. "But we don't have to worry about something like that, do we?"

Nikki felt Gelu's eyes on her, and she swallowed. "Of course not."

The pilot gave a signal that it was safe to disembark, and Sadal got up, swung open the door. Warm air blasted in.

Zakir reached for her hand. "Come then, Nikki. Let me welcome you to my palace."

Staff were rushing forward over the grass, pushing a stretcher for Samira, bending low as the swirling blades came to a stop.

Sweat prickled under Nikki's robes. Little did Zakir know that by taking her into his Summer Palace he had probably set in motion his own downfall.

He led her through a high arch of pink stone. A massive set of gates clanged shut behind them, armed sentries moving back into position.

No way in.

And no way out.

Returning to the Summer Palace was difficult for Zakir. He'd been a mere teen—not much older than Samira—the last time he'd visited this place. And memories snaked up now, baring fangs at him at inopportune moments, rattling him a little.

Agitatedly, he paced in the great study as he dialed Tariq's number. This office had been his father's—marble floors and columns, a sweeping desk of carved mahogany, a bank of LCD security screens and electronics hidden behind gilt doors. It functioned as a high-tech nerve hub and war room, with the black granite table at the center large enough to accommodate the twelve generals of the Sheik's Army and key members of the Council.

"Zakir?" Worry bit into Tariq's rich voice as he answered the phone. "Have you had another episode?"

"I'm fine, but I do need you to do something for me, Tariq."

That icicle of doubt had not left Zakir. He remained uncomfortable with the way Nikki had so visibly paled at the idea of the Council investigating her past.

She might not have entered his country with intention to harm him, but after talking with her outside the tent in the Rahm Hills he believed she *was* hiding something. And he couldn't afford surprises.

It hadn't mattered at the time, but now that he'd gone and tied his own future to her, he needed to know what it was that she wanted kept secret. Her past had suddenly, and inadvertently, become his problem. And his country's problem. And if there was a nasty skeleton in her closet, Zakir needed to know what it was before his enemies did.

Hopefully he hadn't made a very grave mistake in giving her name as his betrothed to the King's Council. And deep down he was furious with himself for once again having been swayed by his libido.

Zakir cleared his throat. "I have one name on my short list already, Tariq—Nikki Hunt. A nurse from the States. I need you to initiate a private background check on her. For the past six years she's been working for Mercy Missions at a remote outpost in Mauritania. She recently entered Al Na'Jar seeking safe passage to the coast for a group of war orphans following a rebel attack on her mission."

"*She* is someone you're interested in, Zakir? A *mission nurse?*"

Zakir heard the surprise—amusement, even—in his brother's voice, and it made him wince inwardly. Not even Tariq knew the extent of the inner change this pending blindness had wrought in him or how he was reevaluating life as he reconnected with this old country. Or how the sheer gravity of the work that lay ahead daunted him and how he was yearning for a true partner with whom to share his burden and his life.

"It's purely a business arrangement," he countered. "The Council is already vetting her, Tariq."

"You have declared her? This sounds serious, brother."

Zakir inhaled, his worry deepening. "I need to know before our enemies do if there are any skeletons in Ms. Hunt's closet. And I need to know fast. Can you coordinate this for me?"

"Of course," said Tariq. "I'll contact our investigative division right away. I'll call you as soon as we have anything on her."

"Shokrun, ya akhi." Thank you, my brother.

"The Berbers are aligning with him." Gelu spoke quietly into his satellite phone. "He's stabilizing the entire eastern region, building grassroots support."

"And this woman? This sudden betrothal to that nurse?" He heard the anger in his handler's voice. "What in hell is going on there? I thought she was working for you?"

Gelu wiped sweat from his brow. "I have her under control. She has moved into the Summer Palace, along with her orphans. She now has even better access to the king. I can use this."

"He cannot be allowed to marry her. He'll become too powerful. He'll change the constitution and immediately start the shift toward democracy, as his father had been threatening to. We'll lose *everything*. Including the oil reserves." Urgency bit into his handler's voice. "What happened to that 'accident' you were going to arrange for him in the Rahm Hills?"

"The woman thwarted us. She persuaded the king to go alone with her into the hills."

His handler swore. "And now look where we are—he's

gone and unified the peasants. We'll have to mobilize the insurgency to that region now."

Gelu's mouth was dry. He felt the tables turning. He could see that he'd end up being the scapegoat if this mission failed. His handler, on the other hand, would remain untouched, as would his handler's powerful puppet masters pulling strings from somewhere else in the world. Gelu had no idea who they were. He cared only that he got a paycheck.

"If we cannot find a reason to challenge Al Arif's throne before he takes a queen, there remains only one way to seize power." His handler's voice turned flat, cool. Quiet. "The king must die." He paused, allowing this to sink in.

"Find a way to do it without any blame falling back on you whatsoever. If you become a suspect, it *will* lead back to us. That cannot happen. We'll kill you ourselves before that happens. Understood?"

"Understood."

"Meanwhile, we'll see if we can dig up any dirt on this woman."

Gelu signed off, sweating profusely. He was in the olive grove, far from the castle, where it was dark and quiet. He walked slowly among the gnarled trunks of the old trees, dry leaves crunching softly underfoot.

How on earth was he going to assassinate the king at the summer fortress and make it look like an accident—without witnesses, without blame pointing to him? The Rahm Hills had been the perfect opportunity, one he'd lost because of that woman. And the king had gained enormous ground because of it. Because of her.

Gelu stilled in his tracks as an idea suddenly hit him.

It was dark when Zakir abandoned his study, and his vision was once again weak. He walked slowly down the palace halls, his boot heels echoing on marble, three dogs by his side.

All through his life Zakir had sought to control things, fix things, take the things he wanted. But against this genetic trait that had been passed down through the dynasty, he was powerless. Vulnerable.

And vulnerability was not an emotion he had learned to cope with.

At least he felt more at peace within the walls of the Summer Palace. And he no longer felt a need to have his Gurkhas moving like shadows at his heels. He was keeping his inner living quarters private, just for him, Nikki and her kids. It would help him relax.

Zakir stopped outside the door to the chambers he'd assigned to the orphans, interleading rooms with beds covered in white Egyptian linen and draped with elaborate netting that hung down from the high ceilings. The bathrooms were of marble and gilt, and outside there was a garden of the children's own, safe behind high turreted walls.

He watched from the main door as Nikki tucked her little united nations platoon into bed in this makeshift nursery, and he'd be damned if it didn't do odd things to his male ego. He'd never wanted children—never even thought about it really, beyond needing an heir. Until now.

Until he watched her.

As if sensing him, Nikki suddenly glanced up and smiled. In this light her features were indistinct, but her pleasure at seeing him lit his heart like a beacon.

He waited until she was done. Closing the door softly behind her, she touched his arm, and the air almost seemed to quiver. "Thank you, Zakir," she said, softly. "It's like a miracle—Samira's contractions have completely stopped."

He smiled, took her arm. "Come," he said gently. "I've asked that our dinner be set out on the main patio tonight, overlooking the central pool."

The dogs drifted behind them like shadows as they walked,

and the sickle moon could be glimpsed through the corridor arches, high above in the Sahara sky.

Zakir led Nikki out onto the patio, where the air felt rounded and soft as velvet on Nikki's skin.

Below the patio lay a dark shimmering rectangle of water, and the moon's reflection shimmered on the surface. Palms rustled in a faint breeze, the air heady with the sweet scent of night blooms. This Summer Palace was like a faraway oasis of calm in an upturned world.

Nikki stilled, overwhelmed suddenly—by the beauty, but even more so by the sense of serenity and safety and the commanding presence of this enigmatic man at her side. To be under his guard at this Moorish palace high in the remote hills of Al Na'Jar was a far cry from her past.

Yet oddly, her past was also coming closer here, and with this thought came a sense of foreboding. She could almost hear the threat whispering in the palm fronds.

"I spoke to Tariq earlier," Zakir said as he held a chair out for her. "I told him about you and your orphans."

Nikki's stomach clenched at the mention of Dr. Al Arif's name. "And?"

"He recommended an obstetrician. I have already sent for her. She's tying up some commitments, but should be here within three or four days."

Relief rushed through her. For tonight, at least, her identity was safe. For tonight she could still pretend she had never been Alexis Etherington.

Take it one day at a time, Nikki, just as you handled the drink. It's all you can do right now.

She watched as Zakir felt for his dogs and his own chair. Her heart went out to him. His vision was clearly worse at night. The guttering flame light from torches that burned in the sconces along the patio walls were probably no help, either.

"You have no electricity outdoors," she noted.

He smiled. "No. My father preferred the torches. He said it reminded him of nights out in the desert."

"You were very fond of him, weren't you?"

"Yes. Very much so. We were—are—a close family."

"Why have you never married, Zakir?" she asked suddenly. "Why not a family of your own?"

He sat quiet for a moment. Palms rustled softly.

"I almost did marry once, long ago," he said finally, very quietly. "But my fiancée was not who she appeared to be."

"How so?"

"Sometimes fortune and power is not all it's cracked up to be, Nikki. Sometimes it's tough to tell friend from foe. Or opportunist. Sometimes you don't really make true friends at all."

Nikki was quiet for a moment. "So she was after your money?"

"Yes."

"But you loved her?"

"It was a mistake." He snorted softly. "I kept my relationships superficial from that point. And the more women I dated, the more effortless it all became. I actually began to enjoy it. The variety, the conquests. It made me feel alive."

"So basically you slept around?"

"Well—" He smiled mischievously. "It was good for my health. At least in that one instance. It saved my life."

She studied his profile in the torchlight. So regal. So authoritative. Yet tonight, somehow so alone.

"Will you change it?"

"My relationships?"

She laughed. "No. The torches. Will you bring electricity out here?"

Again he was pensive for a while. "No," he said quietly. "I

don't believe I will." He reached out in the warm darkness as he spoke and touched her hand.

A lump caught in her throat. It was as if Zakir needed her. As if touching her reassured this powerful man in some way that he'd be okay when the total darkness, the blindness inevitably came. And with shock Nikki realized she, too, wanted *his* touch. She *needed* to be loved again. To be cared for. To somehow be forgiven for all she'd done wrong in her life.

She hungered for this catharsis, this absolution, just as deeply as she feared being exposed. And it scared the hell out of her.

Because Nikki realized she'd just crossed a line of no return.

She was falling for the king.

Chapter 12

Samira was unable to contain her excitement. The fourteen-year-old rested on a chaise longue alongside the pool under the shade of a massive palm, hydrated, nourished, well-rested and looking beautiful in a robe of shimmering greens and violets that Zakir had provided for her. But the true source of Samira's contagious energy and smiles was the books that surrounded her—all written in French.

When Samira had first arrived at the mission she'd surprised Nikki with her command of languages, and Nikki had learned that Samira's father had been the village schoolteacher before her community was slaughtered. The books at the mission quickly became Samira's escape from the horrors of her young life, but after the rebel attack and their flight into the Sahara, she hadn't read a word, and the haunted look in Samira's eyes had returned.

Seeing the exuberance back in her features now was beyond heartwarming to Nikki.

The younger children, too, were happy, and simply being

children, splashing in the pool with a ball. Nikki was almost afraid to allow herself to feel the sheer depths of her joy as she watched the orphans play.

It could all be gone one in the blink of an eye. Like her twins.

The dark memory brought the image of Tenzing Gelu to mind. Nikki hadn't seen him since Zakir had relegated his personal bodyguards to the outer areas of the palace, keeping the living quarters private. She hoped it would stay that way. She promised herself she'd tell Zakir about Gelu as soon as she and the children were safely in Tenerife.

One day at a time. One step at a time. Like the way you made your way over the burning sands of the Sahara. It's all you can do.

And Nikki slowly allowed herself to slide into the warmth of this moment and just be. She, too, was wearing a robe fit for a medieval desert princess, with wide sleeves and cool fabric. Over her hair she wore a veil fringed with tiny shimmering crystal beads that tinkled softly when she moved. A book rested idly in her hands. She closed her eyes, feeling the warmth, just listening to the children laugh.

But they flew open when she heard Zakir's voice call out a greeting to the kids.

He came striding along the side of the pool, tall, hair glinting blue-black in the sun, his hounds trotting at the heels of his black riding boots. She smiled, pleasure surging through her chest as he approached.

With his gleaming hair and finely chiseled features, he looked like the cover of a magazine. She could imagine him in Europe, with his private jets and fast cars and fast women. Yet she was learning that there was so much more to him.

He grinned as he came up to her, his teeth stark white against his dusky complexion, and Nikki's breath caught low in her chest.

"Zakir."

"I see the children are happy, and Samira—" he turned to address the smiling teen *"—ça va bien?"*

"Très bien, merci." She grinned. "Thank you for all the books."

And Nikki's heart expanded further. How could she feel so much happiness? It almost made her guilty, as if she was somehow neglecting the tragedy of her twins' deaths.

The images of that snowy Christmas Eve hit her again.

Cold.

Ice.

The gut-sickening sensation of her car being hit by the black SUV, then hit again. The terrifying realization that someone was trying to run her off the bridge, the raw horror of losing control, sliding. Going through the bridge barrier. The crunch of metal as she slammed into the highway below, the nauseating spinning and folding of metal and breaking glass as the truck hit them. Lying in the street. Bleeding. Fading in and out of consciousness. Chase crying. Hailey deadly silent. Flashing ambulance, police lights.

The images assaulted her like a punch to the stomach, and Nikki felt a chill despite the warm sun. And right on the back of the nausea came a deluge of anger that pumped fire into her veins.

She clenched her hands, her jaw.

She did *not* want to think about what came next.

This was why she'd come to Africa. To lose herself in the hot, dry, open desert. To forget. To heal those who could not heal themselves as she had been unable to heal herself.

Zakir's brows lowered. "Are you all right, Nikki?"

"I'm fine." She forced another smile, grasping desperately for something with which to change the subject. "Your dogs… they've been groomed." She reached out to stroke Khaya's silky fur. "They really are beautiful animals, Zakir."

His frown deepened as he watched her. "Bred in the finest of desert tradition," he said. "The Bedouins call the saluki 'wind drinker' or 'eye of the desert' because of their speed and endurance and because they hunt by sight, not scent." He was studying her intently, his ink-black eyes naked today. Mesmerizing.

"Is that why you got the salukis, to hunt?"

Something shifted in his features. He didn't answer. Instead, he said, "Have you ever seen a saluki in action, Nikki?"

"I have not."

"It's quite a sight to behold. Do you ride?"

She laughed. "I ride camels. Had to learn that pretty fast."

He grinned. "I mean horses."

She hesitated. "It's…been a while since I've ridden a horse."

"How long?"

Too long. Over seven years long. She glanced away.

He thrust his hand out to her. "Come with me, Nikki. My dogs need some exercise and practice, and I need a break from politics. I will show you how they hunt."

Being back in the saddle came easily to Nikki, and it disturbed her to see how simply one could slide into past habits. But as she trotted on a white Arabian mare behind Zakir's gleaming black stallion, Nikki felt the shackles of concern slipping away as the freedom of the desert and vast sky coursed into her blood again. She nudged her mare into a canter until she rode side by side with Zakir across the plain toward a low ridge to the west.

They slowed to climb a steep and rocky trail, and as they crested, Zakir reined in his black horse atop the ridge.

Far away in the distance, over miles and miles of rolling red and gold hills, was a glimpse of cobalt along the horizon.

"The Atlantic," he said as she came to a halt beside him, her mare's tail flicking.

A sense of awe rolled over Nikki. "It's so beautiful up here," she whispered.

He studied her, his obsidian eyes intense, black hair loose on his shoulders. The hooded peregrine falcon tethered to his gauntleted arm shifted, and the bells on the raptor's feet chinked as it moved, the small diamonds set into its leather hood winking in sunlight.

"Is it the kind of freedom you found in the sands of the Sahara, Nikki?"

Her horse shifted under her, and Nikki moistened her lips. His question intrigued her. It was personal. "It's vast and beautiful, Zakir, but it's still within the guarded perimeter of your estate. How can it be the same?"

And oddly, seeing the strip of Atlantic Ocean in the distance made her feel strangely exposed. America was on the other side of that water. She wondered about Sam's potential reach across that sea, what he'd do if he learned she was here. The Al Arif fortress would be no protection against Senator Sam Etherington. Not without Zakir's will to protect her.

And Nikki knew if she was exposed as the runaway wife of a powerful U.S. senator, Zakir would have to act. He'd have no choice but to make an example of her, to follow the laws of his country. Or hers, if Sam pushed for extradition.

And now Zakir had gone and put her name before his council. If they found her out, Nikki's downfall would become Zakir's. And the fall of his country.

He would never forfeit his kingdom for her.

Her false identity was a ticking time bomb. She couldn't do this to him. She had to leave before it exploded. Samira's contractions had miraculously stopped, and the baby was still eight weeks out—she should tell Zakir they were ready to go. Maybe even by morning.

Nikki's mare edged under her again and snorted.

The animal was twitchy, impatient, picking up on her tension. Like her, the animal needed to run. Again.

"Are you ready, Nikki?"

His words caught her off guard. "For what?"

A wicked grin slashed across his face, and his eyes twinkled devilishly. "The hunt!"

Nerves rustled through her. "Of course I'm ready."

He removed the falcon's hood and tether, and raising his gloved arm high, he sent the raptor into the air. The bird swooped upward in a hot flutter of wings, soaring high into the clear, blue sky.

The salukis stiffened instantly, quivering with coiled tension as they fixated on the movements of the raptor above.

The falcon reached a thermal of air and drifted, wings motionless as its keen eyes scanned for prey.

"What is it looking for?" she asked, shading her eyes as she squinted up into the sky.

"In the old days when game was still plentiful in the Sahara, the bird would be searching for oryx or a herd of gazelle. But drought and warmer temperatures over the years have left the sands barren of larger game. Now," he said, watching the raptor, "we are hunting hare. When the falcon begins to fly in wide circles, that's when the salukis will know it has found game." Zakir shot her a glance. "Then they run like the wind until they sight the prey themselves and chase it down."

Her mare whinnied, shifting impatiently again. "And us?"

"We will try to match their speed and endurance." He grinned, telegraphing a crackling kinetic energy, the same kind of barely leashed power she could sense in the dogs as they watched the peregrine soar. Her heart beat faster, and her mouth turned dry. The adrenaline was infectious.

Suddenly the bird changed direction, swooping toward

the peaks, and it began to circle slowly, high in the sky, miles away.

Zakir whistled, and the salukis exploded like bullets from a gun, puffs of red dirt kicking up behind them. He slapped his stallion on the rump, with his right hand. "Yah!" His horse reared, hooves pawing the air. Zakir laughed. And then the animal dropped down into a breakneck gallop after the hounds.

Zakir's hair and robes billowed out behind him as he bent low, riding as if one with horse, red dust boiling in the wake of his black stallion's thudding hooves.

Adrenaline pounded into Nikki's blood. She kicked her own horse into action, racing after Zakir along the top of the ridge, the bells on her saddle chinking, her gauzy veil tearing free from her hair and blowing to the wind. But there was just no way she could keep pace with the sure-footed gallop of Zakir's black stallion, nor could he keep up with his salukis. The hounds ran in a blur, like cheetahs—effortless and elegant—as the peregrine soared above.

He reined his horse suddenly, spinning around to wait for her. The coat of the stallion glistened with perspiration, and Zakir's chest rose and fell with exhilaration.

Breathless, her skin damp, blood thudding in her ears, Nikki came to a stop next to him.

"You doing okay?"

"God, yes." She laughed in release. "I haven't ridden like this in years." She caught her breath. "Actually, I've never ridden like this."

Zakir stilled suddenly, his features turning dark and serious. And Nikki realized she'd lost her veil, that he was looking at her hair. No, not looking—absorbing her, completely. Savoring her.

His horse snorted, tail flicking. And she felt her cheeks grow warm.

"I haven't seen you laugh before, Nikki," he said very quietly.

"It's…been a while since I've felt this…happy."

"A long while?"

She swallowed. "Too long."

He nodded, but his features remained inscrutable. His stallion reared up again abruptly, snorting, and this time he laughed, a deep wild bass that emanated from the depths of his chest. The sound washed over Nikki, stirring something deep inside her.

Mounted on that horse, laughing, his hair loose, Zakir looked untamed yet aristocratic. He reminded her of the paintings of the ancient warrior kings of his country—desert raiders from a time past. It was as if he'd ridden out from one of those oils and come to life in front of her.

He pointed suddenly. "There! Look, Nikki—the dogs have sighted the game. The ground chase has begun! You are ready to ride?"

Nikki grinned, collecting her horse, her heart beginning to thud with excitement all over again. "Hell, yes, I'm ready!"

Taking off at a wild gallop, they charged along the ridge, dropping back down into the plain after the trio of salukis bearing down on the prey.

For miles they charged across the dry plain dotted with sparse scrub, then Nikki saw the hare, a brown blur that made a dash to the right. It was quickly headed off by Ghorab, who channeled the animal back toward Tala. Again the rabbit darted in a different direction, but Tala funneled it back.

It was Khaya who finally clamped down on the animal's throat with her powerful jaws.

Breathless, Nikki caught up to Zakir and the dogs.

He dismounted in a fluid movement, powerful as a black panther. "Come," he said, reaching up for her.

He helped her down off the horse. "This—" he explained

as he motioned for Khaya to release the animal from her jaws and picked up the terrified rabbit by the scruff of its brown neck "—is why we use salukis, Nikki."

The whites of the hare's eyes showed huge and terrified, its little heart hammering against its chest. Zakir unsheathed his jambiya as he spoke, and Nikki tensed as the blade winked in the sun.

"The dogs are trained not to kill the prey because this must be accomplished by the hunter himself, with a knife. In the traditional way, with a clean slice across the neck, here—" He brought the blade to the terrified animal's neck, and Nikki's breath caught in her throat.

"You…you're not going to kill it, are you?"

"It's a hunt, Nikki."

She caught his eyes, unsure if he was serious.

But instead of cutting the hare's neck, Zakir crouched down and gently set the animal back onto the sand. It remained stunned for a nanosecond, then it kicked off, zigzagging into the scrub.

Breath escaped her in an angry whoosh. "You were toying with me, Zakir!"

He stepped up to her, a wicked smile ghosting his sculpted lips, his dark eyes dancing with an exhilaration she found infectious in spite of her fury.

She'd just witnessed Zakir in his prime, spirited and confident on his horse. Happy. How would he be when his vision was gone? Would he miss this?

The thought saddened her. And before she could stop herself, Nikki reached up and gently touched the side of his face.

He stilled.

Unable to stop herself, Nikki moved her hand slowly, exploring the angular shape of his jaw, the suppleness of his dusky skin. Gently, she slid her fingers over his eyes.

She felt one of his dogs brush against her skirt.

Eye of the desert.

"That's why you got the salukis, didn't you, Zakir?" she whispered. "It's not for the hunt, but so that they can be your eyes."

Silence thrummed. Anger twisted into his features, his pulse increasing at his neck. A wariness crept into Nikki. She'd just confronted this powerful sheik with his deepest secret. His Achilles' heel.

But she had to do it. She could not pretend any longer. Zakir was awakening feelings she hadn't experienced for a long, long time, and she was unable to ignore them—or him. "I've seen it in your actions, Zakir," she said softly.

"I saw it in the way you stumbled back at the palace before we left for the Rahm Hills. And in your relationship with your dogs, the way you reach for them, how you need them more at dusk—"

He gripped her wrist hard. Silencing her.

The muscle at his jaw pulsed faster, his eyes narrowing, fierce, glittering. The strength in his grip was phenomenal. Suddenly, she was scared, fisting her hand as she tensed her arm to pull away.

But he held her fast, up against his body. Wind soughed through the scrub, and the falcon's feathers rustled as it came in to land. Bells chinked as it settled on the high horn of Zakir's Moorish saddle. And very slowly he lifted her fisted hand back to his face and forced open her fingers. He pressed her palm flat against the side of his temple and leaned into her touch.

Emotion surged through Nikki, bringing tears to her eyes. She could feel the tension thrumming inside him.

"I am going blind, Nikki," he whispered finally.

The revelation was raw, volatile, and it rocked them both. Nikki had expected him to deny it.

"I…" She swallowed. "I am so sorry, Zakir."

He nodded, shutting his eyes, a tangible sense of relief shuddering through him, as if by sharing this burden he'd released the unbearable tension of keeping this secret private.

"No one else knows, do they, Zakir?"

"No," he said softly in Arabic. "Only my sister and my two brothers and an ophthalmic specialist in Chicago with whom Tariq consults on my behalf. It is a genetic fault in the men of my family that affects every third generation or so."

She'd guessed right—Zakir had Naveed's Hereditary Optic Neuropathy, the same condition Tariq had been studying when he'd approached her at the medical convention all those years ago. Compassion ripped through Nikki's chest. She traced the side of his face with her fingertips, looking deeply and openly into his eyes with the knowledge of a doctor—her own secret she couldn't divulge. But she burned to tell Zakir now. It was no longer right to withhold the truth from him.

"Zakir—"

He silenced her by placing two fingers over her lips. Zakir didn't want to talk about his disability. The sense of catharsis that punched through him as Nikki looked up into his eyes was enough. And her features were suddenly so unguarded, so open, so beautiful, her touch so full of care that it cracked open his control.

He wanted her. All of her. Now.

Forever.

And the urge to sink himself between her legs and claim her, right here in this desert under the open, bright sky surged so powerfully through his blood that he began to shake. He inhaled sharply, feeling as though he was going to implode with the desire to be one with her, to share everything, to no longer be alone.

"Tell me," he whispered hoarsely, "that I have not made a

terrible error in judgment in revealing this to you, Nikki. Tell
me I can trust you. Tell me you will never betray me."

Her answer was to lean up, cup the back of his head and
draw his lips down toward hers.

Zakir thrust his fingers into her tangle of curls and fiercely
crushed his mouth down on hers. Her body sagged for an
instant, and he caught her weight at the small of her back,
yanking her into his arms, feeling her pelvis press against his
arousal. It drove him wild.

Her lips opened warmly under his, and a small sound of
pleasure came from her chest as she felt his tongue enter
her mouth. A rush of aggressive passion seemed to surge
through her body and she moved hungrily, kissing him back,
her breaths coming short and fast. Zakir slid his hands lower,
cupping her buttocks and pulling her skirt up her thigh until
his fingers met flesh. For an instant he couldn't breathe—or
see. But as she hooked her naked leg up around his thigh, she
bumped his sheathed scimitar, and it jolted him back.

He didn't really want to take her out here in the desert, in
the sand. As much as he would relish the wildness of it, he
wanted her in his chambers, naked on his bed, with sunlight
streaming in over her body spread before him.

He wanted to treat her like a princess…like his queen. He
wanted to love her all night long. And again when the sun
rose over his estate.

"Come," he whispered against her mouth, his hand feeling
the delicious silk of her panties as he spoke, the dampness of
her desire. His heart began to race even faster, and the vision
in his left eye began to blur. "Come back with me to the palace
and to my bed."

Chapter 13

They rode fast over the hills, their hearts pounding—a race as urgent as it was playful. Zakir's dogs flowed with fleet-footed grace alongside the horses as the falcon soared above, following them.

When they arrived at the stables, Zakir left the horses and his bird to the experienced care of the palace grooms and dedicated falconer, and they moved quickly to his private quarters.

His chambers were extensive—marble arches opening out onto a private walled garden complete with lush blooms, an oasislike pool and a waterfall. Dates, grapes, almonds and honey had been placed on a table outside under the shade of a lemon tree, along with jugs of minted water. A stained-glass dome rose in the ceiling. Zakir's bed was positioned under the dome and sunlight streamed down through the colored glass, painting a rainbow of light over the white Egyptian linens.

Down a corridor off the room, behind a heavy mahogany door, lay his private study.

But the sumptuous grace of the private chambers was lost on both of them as Zakir hurriedly, breathlessly backed Nikki onto his ornately carved bed.

She fell back onto the linen, hair splaying out around her, and Zakir stilled suddenly.

Malaak er-ruhmuh.

An angel.

And to Zakir, that was exactly what she looked like—her tangle of strawberry-blond curls spreading in a halo around her head as the colored rays of sun streamed down through the stained-glass dome above her.

The image stole his breath away.

How was it that he was so lucky to have this woman just walk into his life at a time he so urgently needed an ally—and a queen?

Or was it more than fate?

Again that icicle of unease pricked cool and deep into his gut, but he shoved the sensation aside. Why should he *not* be lucky?

Why must he always be so suspicious?

Zakir felt in his heart that this woman was good, pure. He'd sensed it the way she'd touched his face. He'd glimpsed the depths of tenderness in her eyes. He'd seen just how far she'd go for her orphans. And to save an old Berber shepherd.

He edged onto the bed beside Nikki, propping himself up with one elbow, leaning closer. Her eyelids fluttered as if she anticipated that he was going to kiss her again. But he didn't.

Instead, he reached for the braided cords and ribbons that secured the front of her robe, and slowly he began to pull them free.

"Oyoon el waha," he whispered as he slid the fabric back from her breasts, exposing them to the glowing light from above. "Eyes of the oasis," he murmured. "I have never seen

eyes like yours, Nikki." He unclasped her bra, and her breasts swelled free, dusky rose nipples tightening under his touch. She inhaled sharply as he gently pinched a nipple between his fingertips, and her cheeks flushed with pleasure.

Molten desire surged between Zakir's thighs at her response, and his breath became lighter, faster. With it came a whisper of worry, because as sexual urgency increased in Zakir's body, so did his pulse rate…and the dark blur in his left eye.

You need to stay calm…

He ignored the warnings in his head as he leaned over her. He was going to go blind anyway. If making love to Nikki meant there was a chance he could savor and commit this vision of her naked on his bed to his memory, he'd take it. Because he'd be able to recall it during his dark days and relive it forever.

She shivered slightly as he trailed his fingers over the swell of her breasts, tracing a line slowly down the center of her abdomen, peeling back the fabric of her robe as he went.

Zakir absorbed every visual detail—the way her bare breasts rose and fell with each breath, the way her lids dipped over her eyes as she felt him touch her, the way her lips were swollen, glossy from their kiss, and parted.

Zakir circled the inside of her belly button with his fingertips. Her eyes darkened with lust on a sharp intake of breath. It fired him. Made him want to move quickly, take her hard and fast. But he bit down on his urgency as he trailed his fingers, ever so slowly, to the hem of her silk panties. She began to tremble, and her eyes suddenly filled with moisture.

"Zakir—"

He stopped. "What is it, Nikki?"

"I…" She closed her eyes. "It's nothing."

"You haven't been with a man for a long time, have you, Nikki?"

"No," she whispered on a breath.

She was like a virgin, nervous, yet he'd tasted the rawness of her sexual hunger, her capacity for fun, her boldness. This dichotomy excited Zakir to an aching pitch.

He was an experienced lover. His goal had always been to hunt, seduce and then to please a woman physically. And he wanted it to be good for Nikki. He wanted her to cry for more, to need him all over again. And again. His arousal throbbed at the mere thought of her opening her thighs for him, arching her pelvis to him, aching for him.

She placed her hand over his suddenly, firmly urging him to move faster, farther into her panties as she kept her eyes closed. He slid his fingers under the silky fabric as he whispered against her mouth. "I will be gentle, Nikki. I will do nothing you don't want. You can tell me to stop anytime—" But Zakir's hand stilled as his fingertips met a thin ridge of a scar across her pubic bone. Nikki stiffened.

He glanced up at her face, and tears began to roll softly from the corners of her closed eyes, into her hair.

"Nikki?" he whispered, bending his head down and gently kissing away the tears, his heart aching even as every nerve in his body was screaming to take her right this minute. Because Zakir knew what the scar was—it was from a C-section.

Nikki had had a child.

And that child wasn't with her now. Which meant it was either somewhere else or she'd lost it.

And suddenly all Zakir could think about was how desperately she was trying to save other people's lost children. Something deep was going on inside Nikki. Something in her past had changed her fundamentally. This was the thing she might be trying to hide.

"Nikki," he whispered again. "Do you want me to stop?" She shook her head angrily, grasped his hand and moved it lower into her panties, between her thighs. She was hot. Wet.

She opened her legs to him. "Please," she murmured, kissing him harder, guiding his fingers between her legs, guiding him inside. She gasped as his fingers entered her. "Please...don't stop." And as he moved his fingers inside her heat, she kissed him—hungry, desperate, arching into his touch even as the tears streamed down her face, and her body moved hungrily, urgently, angrily against his.

He quickly removed her skirt, sliding the fabric off her body. Her skin was smooth, firm, supple. Pale. And quietly Zakir noted another scar—a whorl of angry tissue that ran all the way down the side of her hip to the outside of her knee. And another across the inside of her ankle. He didn't say anything.

But it shifted something inside him.

It burned a powerful compassion into his lust, a desire to nurture, care. Heal. To love her. To make her whole again.

It made what they were doing feel serious, precious, something not to be taken lightly.

Zakir stripped off his own clothes. The sun was warm on his skin as he positioned himself between her thighs and eased his weight over her, coaxing her legs open wide with his knees. He paused, controlling himself. Then slowly, as he watched her eyes, he entered her with just the tip of his erection. She leaned up toward him, her legs opening wider, trembling. He slowly slid in. She caught her breath, her lips parting and eyes going wide as her body accommodated to his size. Her fingers dug into his back, and he felt her grow hotter, wetter, her muscles quivering around his erection.

He slid out, penetrated again, thrusting just a little harder, easing a fraction deeper as he felt her melting and burning around him. She began to move urgently, her breathing faster and lighter as she arched her back, and her skin turned damp.

Trying to control himself became almost unbearable, his

vision swirling to shades of scarlet and black as he thought he might implode. Zakir couldn't last.

Nikki felt him pull out suddenly, and she could feel air and the warmth of sun on the exposed dampness between her legs. Zakir's dark gaze met hers, intense. Then he raked his eyes slowly, pointedly over her breasts, then down to her belly, to her open legs. His breathing came faster. His dark skin glowed in the sunlight, and Nikki's gaze followed the dark whorl of hair from his navel to where it flared deliciously between his very powerful thighs. His erection was glistening, wet. She couldn't breathe.

Leaning forward, she reached out to him, taking his hand, drawing him back down over her. He used his knees to brusquely widen his access. He slid his hands under her buttocks, lifting her pelvis, and with a sudden, hard thrust, he reentered, pushing all the way to the hilt.

She gasped, arched her pelvis up against his, her nails digging into his back and shattered with a cry, the rolling contractions seizing hold of her body, her breath, her mind.

Her release seemed to crack Zakir's control, and he plunged into her repeatedly. Then with one final deep thrust, a shuddering release ripped through his entire body.

They lay coupled under the shafts of colored sunlight, him softening inside her, yet each time she stirred, she felt him come alive between her legs. Nikki had not felt so content, so right, in a long, long time. It was as if sex with Zakir had brought the past into the present in a way that had made her whole again, and Nikki never wanted to let him go.

He murmured words of Arabic against her skin, in her hair, kissing her. "You are so beautiful, Nikki," he said as he stroked her body, tracing each line, each curve. "I want to remember this, how you look."

But then his fingertips touched the scar along her pubic

bone again, and his hand lingered. Nikki felt blood drain from her face.

Their conversation in the Rahm Hills sifted into her mind.

I've never had children, Zakir.

Would he see the scar for what it was—evidence of a lie?

When the denial had come out of her mouth up in those hills, not in her wildest dreams had Nikki ever imagined she'd end up naked in front of the sheik. The scar hadn't even entered her mind. Conflict twisted painfully in her chest. She and Zakir had just shared so much. He had confessed his deepest secret and given her his complete trust. And now Nikki so badly wanted to go all the way and give him hers.

Her stomach clenched.

The more she began to care for him, the more urgently she needed to get away from him. Because each minute was braiding her past more insidiously into his future.

She needed to leave Al Na'Jar—there was no other way out. As much as she suddenly wanted to be with this incredible man, to be loved by him, she had to give him reason to stop this pretense at an engagement. He was only doing it to help her, so she and her children could be here at the Summer Palace with him.

If she told him that Samira's contractions had gone and that they were ready to leave, Zakir could end this betrothal sham before the King's Council investigators got something on her.

And then once she was safely out of the country with her kids she could tell him about the traitor in his inner circle. The sooner he knew about Gelu, the better, too.

He moved his hand around her hip and began to trace his fingers over the ugly scar down the side of her thigh. Nikki's mouth went dry. She could literally feel the questions welling inside him as he explored her body, exposing dark memories with each touch, those chilling images warring with the sensuous warmth of his hands.

As he fingered the outside of her knee, where surgeons had operated and put in a pin, she felt herself closing off. Spiraling away. Her mind already escaping on that boat to Tenerife, thinking how she could be gone by morning.

"How did you get these scars, Nikki?" he said softly.

"It…was a car accident. Nothing serious."

"It feels very serious."

But before he could ask any more questions she got up quickly and went into the bathroom.

Nikki exhaled deeply, splashing cool water over her face. She raked damp fingers through her hair and stood naked in front of the floor to ceiling mirrors.

She studied herself dispassionately, tentatively touching the C-section scar across her pubic area. The scar that had given birth to Hailey and Chase. Tears threatened, and she angrily blinked them back.

Nikki was lousy with emotional pain. She'd dealt with the deaths of her children in the worst possible way, and she had no intention of reliving the agony. Or the downward spiral.

But Zakir was making her feel it all again. The urge to flee suddenly swelled even more fiercely and determinedly in her.

She'd tell him now, before it was too late. Before she brought both their worlds crashing down around them.

Nikki spun around, grabbed a robe from the back of the door. Belting the silk tightly across her waist, she hesitated, sucked in a breath, then exited the bathroom.

"Zakir, I—" Words fled from her as she saw him lying back on the bed, buck naked, his arm hooked under his head. He was watching her intensely while a smile curved wickedly at the corners of his mouth.

His erection stirred as she neared, and his smile deepened. "You see what you do to me, Nikki?"

She swallowed, losing her train of thought, disturbed by the way her own body was already reawakening, stirring at the sight of his sexual arousal. Making her want him again. Making her need him.

She didn't want to feel like this.

Zakir got up suddenly, even more powerful in dark nakedness than clothed with a scimitar at his hip. He came toward her, black hair falling loose on shoulders, supple Mediterranean skin gleaming in the sunlight, the dark hair on his chest tapering into a sensual line to his navel and then flaring out lower at his pelvis.

He held his hand out to her. "Come outside with me, Nikki," he spoke softly, rolling his Arabic words into a sensual murmur.

She hesitated.

But he took her hand anyway. "Come into the sun with me, come swim in my pool."

Nikki did not trust herself to speak as she allowed the king to lure her into his private garden.

He stepped into the pool and ducked under the surface of the water, coming up with droplets sparkling on his skin, his dark hair slicked back and his black eyes laughing.

He made love to her again under the waterfall, and they lay naked under the blue sky. She watched the doves in the trees and felt the sun warm her skin.

Nikki never wanted this to end. She wished she could hide in this sensual limbo forever. Safe and far away. But as the sky turned pink and orange, Zakir turned to her and said quietly, "You've had a child, Nikki."

She went cold, dead inside.

Images of the highway, the snow. Her babies, the funerals, the little coffins, the court cases... Nikki inhaled deeply, suddenly distant, unable to speak. She reached for the silk robe, slipped it on and got to her feet.

He stilled her by grasping her hand. "This child is not with you, which means you have…lost it, somehow?"

She bit her lip to stop from letting any emotion out. She nodded in silence, belting the robe, eyes bone-dry, itchy.

He waited, his black eyes burning questions into her, and in his features Nikki read not the anger of a man who'd been lied to but empathy, tenderness.

That was the worst. It made her want to crack and tell him everything, but she couldn't. Not until she was safely out of the country.

"Is this why you save other children?"

She glanced up sharply. Silence hung for several beats. "I… should go check on them, Zakir. I… Samira's contractions have not returned. The baby is still eight weeks away. She… she'll be safe to travel by morning." She sucked air in deep, steeling herself for this new course of action. "If you will give us a pilot and helicopter to take us to the port, it would be easiest on her. From there we'll take a boat, and you can tell the King's Council that the betrothal is over."

His features turned dark.

But before he could say anything, she walked out, pulling the door closed behind her.

Zakir blew out a breath of frustration. But he let her go. He lay back, closed his eyes, swearing softly to himself. He'd tried so hard not to scare her away as he delved into her secrets. He'd tried to make it good for her. It looked as though he'd just failed.

In so many more ways than one.

And now that he'd failed to persuade her to stay of her own accord, he couldn't allow her to go. He could not let her break off this betrothal until his new wife was lined up.

Or he could lose his country.

Chapter 14

For the rest of the afternoon, Zakir attended to pressing military strategy in his office. Two of his army generals had flown in, and together they had discussed the new highly sensitive satellite communications bases that had been covertly installed in the desert. Most of stations were hidden below-ground, in bunkers, and were invisible from the air. But all through the discussion, Zakir's mind was never far from Nikki.

He told himself that it was good to spend time away from her—she needed time alone to digest things. Clearly she'd confronted a milestone in her life—sleeping with a man again. And she'd suffered the deep loss of a child in her past, under circumstances that Zakir could see she was not yet ready to talk about. He argued that this was the only reason she'd said that she wanted to leave tomorrow.

She'd calm down and come to her senses by dinner.

He hoped.

Because if she didn't, he was in a bind. Having his "fiancée" walk out on him was going to create serious credibility problems with the King's Council. He was going to have to find a way to make her change her mind—carefully, with the skill of a military strategist.

If he failed, he'd be left with no choice but to hold her captive for a short while. Until he married someone else.

Or he could lose his throne.

But suddenly, the throne, his country, his future...didn't seem quite as clear without Nikki in it, and Zakir realized he enjoyed being with her more than he'd cared to admit. She was like a bright beacon of promise in the darkness that lay ahead. A light against his looming threat of blindness. He realized he wanted Nikki to stay...because he *needed* her, quite apart from the role she was serving in helping him secure his throne.

This irked him.

As soon as his generals left his office for the guest wing of the palace, Zakir picked up his phone and dialed Tariq.

"Any word on the Nikki Hunt investigation?"

"Not yet," said Tariq.

"She's had a child. Tell the investigators to add that into the mix. There will be birth records somewhere."

He hung up and dialed again, pacing agitatedly as he waited for his emissary in Paris to pick up.

"Zakir," the man said. "I'm pleased you called. I have just finished the interviews and will have the list of the top twenty candidates to you by the end of next week. From there you can select the top ten who will—"

"That will no longer do." He cut the man short. "I want you yourself to pick just the top five tonight and have them on a plane to Al Na'Jar by morning. Arrange for them to stay at the Sahara Sun. And do not breathe a word to the staff at the Sun, nor to any media. No one can know who these women are or why they're in my country."

Especially Nikki. Not after they'd made love. There was

something fragile developing between them, and Zakir didn't want to crush it.

"And they must not communicate with anyone. I'll arrange for a male interpreter. He can speak for them. Understand?"

He signed off, blood pressure high again. And his left eye blurred, then went dark. With shock his right eye started to blur, as well. Zakir gripped the back of his chair and stood still, trying to calm himself until his vision returned. This time it took well over an hour. The episodes were coming closer and closer together. His time was running out.

Late that night while dining under the stars with bright torches flaming in wall sconces, the vision in Zakir's left eye began to fail yet again. A higher dose of medication had done little to help, and fear that total blindness was imminent any hour hovered, circled with the dancing night shadows.

He didn't like the ominous shift he sensed in Nikki's demeanor, either.

Her conversation was cool, stilted, as if she'd shut down, locked him out. Zakir felt hot, irritable, frustrated.

"Do you want to tell me about it, Nikki?"

She glanced up slowly.

Again she'd declined his offer of a glass of fine wine. He wished she would drink—it would relax her, too.

"You mean about my C-section scar?"

He nodded, watching her intently with his right eye as he sipped his wine.

"I lost my child in an accident, Zakir," she said quietly. "I don't want to talk about it, or remember it. And it's not your concern, irrespective of what you say about your country, because I'll be gone by tomorrow."

His pulse kicked and his chest tightened. He set his glass down slowly. "I didn't mean to scare you. Please, stay. It will be better for Samira, and you know it. The obstetrician will be here before long."

"You know a lot about women, don't you, Zakir?" she said quietly.

"Because I know the meaning of such a scar?"

"I don't think every man would recognize it for what it is."

"I'm not every man."

"No. You're not." Her words were crisp. "You're privileged royalty, an international bachelor playboy driven by sexual conquests. I saw the magazine stories, the photos. They call you the tycoon, playboy sheik."

"Where—" his voice was cool, cautious "—did you see these stories?"

"I asked the palace staff for Internet access through the satellite system this afternoon."

"And they *gave* it to you?"

"Why shouldn't they? Am I some sort of prisoner? You've made it public that we are betrothed, Zakir. Your staff thus believes I have your trust. So why should they not trust me, too?"

A dark foreboding began to rise in him. "What did you see, Nikki?" he said, very quietly. "What were you looking for?"

She said nothing.

Several beats of silence passed. Hot wind guttered the flames in sconces, making them crackle, making shadows writhe ominously over the patio. Zakir pressed his fingers to his left temple. "Tell me," he said again, "what you were searching for."

She cast her eyes down for a moment and inhaled deeply. "I haven't read a newspaper in six years, Zakir. I don't know what's going on in the world. And I wanted to see what news there was of Mauritania and the rebel movement there."

And I wanted to see what Sam was up to, where he was now, how much more powerful he might have become. Because you're making my past come closer, and I'm afraid.

"You could have just asked me. I would get you any information you wanted."

"And while on the laptop," she continued, "I…searched your name, on impulse. I wanted to know more about you."

"And?"

She set her napkin carefully on the table. "I saw that you're a serial womanizer, Zakir, with ridiculously extravagant tastes and far too much cash to blow on nightclubs, cars, helicopters, yachts. I saw who you really are—"

"Who I *was*," he snapped. "I have made no secret of this, Nikki. And I am not that man now."

She lifted her eyes slowly, and he sensed a very real vulnerability under her harsh words. Zakir's heart torqued. She cared. *That* was why she'd looked him up.

A whisper of excitement curled through him, braiding with caution. Zakir had to tread very lightly and cleverly here. He did not want to lose her because of old gossip on the Internet. He needed to get her to agree to stay of her own accord.

"And why *have* you have changed, Zakir?"

He reached across the table for her hand. "I told you why, Nikki. Coming back here to the desert, experiencing my heritage—it has shifted something fundamental in me. This on top of the loss of my mother and father, and Da'ud—" He paused. "I have a duty now. I have enemies who must pay. And Nikki," he said, lowering his voice earnestly, "I felt nothing for those women. I loved being with them, yes, but I never got attached to any one of them. Not like now."

"What about now?"

Now I am falling for a most unusual woman, and I don't even really know who she is.

"Now I met you."

Her jaw tensed. "Shall I tell you what I think really changed you, Zakir?"

"By all means, please do." He couldn't stop a sudden irritability from lacing into his tone. He was losing control of a very delicate situation.

She leaned forward, lowering her voice to a whisper. "I think it's your impending loss of vision."

"I am not afraid of the darkness," he replied crisply.

"But you *are* afraid that you could lose your throne because of it. That's why you've gone to such great lengths to hide it from everyone, isn't it? That's why you made me promise, out in the desert while we were hunting, not to tell anyone your 'secret.'"

She hesitated, weighing her next words. "Did you know that one of the Parisian tabloids is claiming breaking news about you?"

"*What* news?"

"Some model apparently leaked a story late this afternoon about being interviewed as a possible wife for you. She told the magazine that you have an agent in Europe who is interviewing women for the role of queen of Al Na'Jar and that just today you sent an order to the agent to cut the search short, select the top five candidates and ship them to Al Na'Jar by morning. The article claimed you would marry one of the five within the next few weeks."

Zakir remained dead quiet, every muscle in his body tense, simmering as he waited for Nikki to finish.

"This model claimed she'd been among the top twenty candidates, and now she's been axed. She claimed you'd reneged on your end of the agreement by doing this, therefore she felt her confidentially clause was null and void. So she took her story to the top bidding tabloid."

Silent fury swelled inside Zakir. So *this* was what had upset

Nikki. His rage, however, was spiked with panic. The closer he came to losing her, the more he wanted her.

And he would *not* lose her.

Not to this nonsense.

"Do you know what else this model told the magazine, Zakir? Apparently, you cannot take the official oath and be sworn in as the king until you are married. *You* told me that the only reason you hadn't taken the official oath was because you'd been preoccupied with stabilizing the unrest in the country. You lied to me, Zakir."

He said nothing, not trusting himself to speak, not wanting to send her off in the wrong direction.

She leaned forward, hurt thickening her voice. "You *used* me. You put my name forward as your fiancée for your own security with the King's Council while you secretly hunted for a bride in Europe. So why *did* you sleep with me? Just another in your string of sexual conquests?" She got to her feet, emotion glittering in her eyes.

"Nikki, please—"

She raised both hands in front of her, shaking her head. "You didn't bring me here for Samira's safety, not at all. You lured me here using the one thing in this world that I care about—my children—just so you could save your goddamn throne. And—" her voice cracked "—and now that you've gone and put my name before your King's Council, and now that I know this secret of yours...*can* you let me go, Zakir? Or are you going to hold me captive while you pick one of those...those models, and you can become king where nothing can touch you...not even blindness?"

He inhaled sharply. She'd pushed him onto a precipice. "Nikki, please, this is not so—"

"Then *prove* it! Allow me to leave. Give me a pilot and a Black Hawk. Fly me and the children *all* the way to Tenerife first thing in the morning." She flung her arm out, pointing west to where the Canary Islands lay.

"Please, sit."

She remained standing, eyes defiant, body rigid.

"I can explain, Nikki. I'll tell you *everything*. No secrets. Nothing more to hide between us." He ran a hand through his hair. "You're right about my fear of losing the throne due to my...issue. And you're correct about me needing a queen in order to become king. As soon as I marry I can unilaterally change any law I choose, and no one will be able to challenge my position. So yes, after my father and Da'ud were assassinated, Tariq, Omair, Dalilah and I decided that it was best if we initiated the interviews in Europe. I hoped to sign an agreement with a woman willing to serve as my queen for a limited period of time until the monarchy was secure. Then...then I met you." Zakir rubbed his brow, searching for the right words. He needed to go back further, to make her understand who he was and why he'd made certain choices in his life.

"Look, you must understand, Nikki. I told you I once loved a woman. I never allowed it to happen again—"

"Why not?" she asked, sitting quietly. "Tell me about this woman."

"It started while I was still studying economics at the Sorbonne in Paris. I was young. She was very beautiful. She said her name was Lara. I dated her for two years, and we got engaged to become married." He reached for his wine, took a deep sip. "Turned out she was a freelance operative—a skilled seductress who sleeps with a target for information, and she'd been hired by a rival corporation that chose to zero in on me because I was the one with a weakness for beautiful women, and I was also next in line to head up a powerful arm of the Al Arif Corporation. They had long-term plans for her. And me."

"Industrial espionage?"

He nodded. "My love for that woman almost cost the entire Al Arif empire. Only a fool makes the same mistake twice. It was a lesson I never forgot, and I could never put my family at risk like that again. I became cynical, overly cautious, suspicious. And this is why I am seeking a wife by this method." He paused, leaned forward, taking her hand.

"But destiny threw me a curveball by putting you on my palace boulevard, Nikki, and...I found something real. Something beautiful that made me question everything. It made me wonder," he said very quietly, "if I could learn to love again, if I might actually be able to marry for affection, as my father did when he married my mother. And you know what? I began to yearn for that. I began to hope, even as the clock ticked down on my blindness, even as I needed to move fast to secure this country, that I might get to know you better, that you might be the person I wanted you to be, before I ran out of time."

Nikki closed her eyes for a moment, her features tight. Moisture glistened under her lashes.

He cupped the side of her face. "Nikki, you are like no one I've ever met." His voice caught on a sudden surge of emotion, becoming hoarse, low. Seductive. "I *want* you, Nikki. I want you to try on the role of queen. Just for a short while. Get to know the real me. And allow me to get to know you. One step, one day at a time."

She slumped a little at these words, leaning into his touch as if desperate to believe, yet still fighting it with every morsel of her being.

"I've seen your love for my desert. I've witnessed your understanding of my people. I have seen your passion and purpose through the way you have protected and cared for your children. It not only makes you more beautiful than any woman I have known. It makes you the perfect role model for this country. My people need you. *I* need you."

A pearl of moisture slid from the corner of her eyes, glistening in flame light as it tracked down her cheek.

He wiped it away with his thumb.

No one had ever said such beautiful things to her, making her feel worthwhile, loved, absolved, things she'd so very deeply craved since the death of Hailey and Chase, since her downward spiral into alcoholic oblivion and her long slow crawl back.

"Those other five women, Nikki, are merely a backup. In case I could not persuade you to stay." He pressed his fingers to his left temple suddenly, closing his eyes for a moment. "I am running out of time," he said quietly. "My vision is failing. And if you insisted on leaving, on breaking off our engagement—"

"I was never actually engaged to you, Zakir. You said it was a pretense so I could be here."

"It's real in the King's Council's eyes."

"So you *did* use me."

"Only because I wanted to know you better. I would have moved more slowly if I could have, Nikki. But I just don't have the luxury of time." He paused. "Can you accept this?"

She cast her eyes down and fidgeted with her napkin, emotions twisting. Zakir was offering her everything she ever wanted—and a chance to fall in love. Then she thought of Gelu, what he might still want of her and the children if she stayed. And of what it could still cost Zakir if her past came out. "Zakir, I can't—"

But before she could finish her sentence, a ruckus sounded outside the doors—guards yelling, footsteps clattering down the hall.

The doors to the patio burst open, and little Solomon came

barreling through, Zakir's Gurkhas close on his heels, trying to stop him from barging in on the king's dinner.

"Miss Nikki, Miss Nikki, *she's gone!*" Tears gleamed over Solomon's brown cheeks.

Nikki lurched from her chair, crouched down, taking his shoulders. "Shh, take it easy, Solomon. *Breathe.*"

He gulped down air.

"Now tell me, who is gone?"

"Samira!"

Tension whipped through her. She flicked a glance at Gelu who was lurking by the door now, his features impassive.

"What do you mean, *gone?*"

"She's not in the room, not in the palace, not anywhere."

Zakir dismissed his guards with a curt wave of his hand and came to Nikki's side. "She must be somewhere on the grounds, Solomon."

He closed his eyes, shook his head. "She would not go anywhere, Miss Nikki, not without telling me. She always tells me everything. She said I was her backup. She said I was brave like her little brother. She promised she'd never leave me alone if she had to go somewhere again." He began to shake. "I just know, Miss Nikki, I do. Someone has taken her. Something *terrible* has happened."

Chapter 15

The younger kids stared in silence as Nikki rummaged wildly through everything in their room, trying to see if Samira had taken clothes, books. But nothing was missing.

She spun round. "Did she say anything to anyone?"

Heads shook.

"Solomon—" Nikki crouched down in front of him, trying to stay calm, keep her voice level, but fear was rising uncontrollably in her chest. Gripping his bony shoulders a little too hard, she asked, "When did you all last see Samira? What was she doing? *Think*."

He scowled, brow lowering, features tightening as he racked his brain. "It was this afternoon," he said in French. "Down past the pool, near the tree plantation—"

"The olive grove?"

He nodded vigorously. "She was talking to someone."

"Who!" Nikki reined herself in when Solomon's eyes went wide and round. She softened her voice. "Who was she with, Solomon?"

"One of the women who comes up from the village to work in the palace kitchen. She's a very nice lady, Miss Nikki... She—" Solomon glanced nervously at the king towering in silence behind Nikki. "She sneaks us fresh dates and guavas when the other kitchen staff aren't looking."

Zakir spun on his boot heels and stalked out of the chambers, boots ringing angrily down the corridor as he headed for the kitchen wing.

By midnight, there was still no sign of Samira.

The woman from the kitchen had been located and questioned by Zakir. She said she knew nothing of what had happened to the teenager. She'd simply been showing Samira how to pick the first ripe blond olives. The woman was trembling, distressed and tearful at having been brusquely interrogated by the king himself, at being thought responsible for the teen's disappearance.

Nikki stood on the edge of the patio in the dark, staring down toward the shadowed olive grove that had been searched twice already by staff. Her mouth was dry, she felt dizzy, cold in spite of the heat.

Zakir came up behind her, touched Nikki on the shoulder and she jumped.

She turned, looked up. The glow from the torches that burned from sconces along the terrace wall danced over the sharp angles of his profile. "She's not here, Zakir. She's gone—something terrible has happened."

"I'm sure she just wandered off, got lost."

Gelu's taken her. I'm sure of it.

"Samira wouldn't do that, Zakir. Not without telling me. Or Solomon. You heard what he said. Samira had a little brother who died in her care. Solomon has become that little brother to Samira now. She'd die before abandoning him."

"We *will* find her," he said gently. "My men are still searching the palace grounds."

"All those miles of it? In the dark?" Nikki clenched her teeth, wrapping her arms tightly over her stomach. "I...I've got to do something, Zakir. I can't just sit all night and wait."

"Nikki," he said softly, "tell me more about Samira, her background. When did she arrive at your mission?"

Nikki inhaled deeply. "The first time she was eleven. Her parents had been killed when her village was attacked. Samira, her younger brother and a few other children had managed to flee. At night they slept in the bush near the village, and during the day they hid from rebels who would otherwise capture them to work as child soldiers or sex slaves. But when her brother cut his foot and developed a serious infection, Samira found her way to the mission for help." Nikki fell silent for a while, trying to compose herself. "Her brother died. We couldn't save him. Samira ran away."

"Why?"

"She didn't trust us. She got spooked by her brother's death. But then...she was raped, violently, by some soldiers, and she was brought back to the mission by a woman who found her bleeding alongside the road." Her voice grew thick. She clutched her arms tighter over her stomach.

"And she has been with you since?"

"She was in real bad shape after the rape, Zakir. When she was somewhat healed, she left one more time. But she returned on her own accord when her pregnancy started to show, and she realized that the mission nurses really might be able to help her bring a baby safely into the world." Nikki wavered. "Which is why I *must* find her, help her."

"Why'd she leave the second time?"

Nikki exhaled. "Samira took a long time to trust, to believe the nurses and priests and sisters at the mission would do right by her. Compassion from strangers was a foreign concept in her life. I also believe she was too young to initially comprehend what pregnancy was going to mean to her. When the gravity of her situation became clear, when she realized she couldn't do this on her own, she returned for help."

"But, you see, Nikki, Samira has a record of going away. Not wanting to be somewhere unless in need. Maybe because she's feeling well again, she might feel there is no longer need to stay here."

Nikki whirled to face Zakir, desperate to tell him about Gelu, about how he'd threatened Samira, but at the same time she was terrified Gelu would find out, and that Samira would bear the consequences. "How?" she demanded, pointing out into the darkness in her frustration. "How would she get out of these grounds—even if she wanted to?"

He grasped her shoulders, steadying her. "Nikki, assassins breached a whole army of trained guards in Al Na'Jar to kill my parents right in their beds. Anything is possible. Samira might have sneaked out with the women from the village who work in the kitchen. They might've told her they could take better care of her than some foreign nurse."

She spun away from him, shaking inside, panic licking through her.

"I am going inside to contact the palace in Na'Jar. I'll bring up another cadre of troops to search the village beyond the palace walls. They'll be here by dawn. They *will* find her. Wherever Samira went, she cannot have gotten far. Not in her condition."

He touched her again as he spoke. But Nikki pulled away, dry eyed. Afraid. Powerless. Frustrated beyond reason. More than any of the other children, Samira was her purpose. Without Samira and her baby, Nikki was cut loose, blowing terrified in the wind. She couldn't even flee the Summer Palace, not without Samira.

She was well and truly trapped now.

"Come inside with me while I make the call."

Nikki shook her head. "I'll wait here."

He hesitated, nodded, then hooked his hand into Ghorab's collar, using his dogs to guide him back through the arches.

Nikki stared fiercely into the darkness, fighting herself. Fighting the anguish that threatened to crash through her and overwhelm all logical thought.

She'd brought Samira so very far, after so many years. She could not stand here doing nothing, just waiting to see if Gelu was going to make a move. Darkness had descended, but she had to keep looking. And she had no idea where to start, other than the point Samira was last seen.

She shot a glance back at the marble arches where flaming torches billowed in the hot desert breeze.

On impulse, she strode to the end of the terrace, took a torch from one of the sconces and descended the wide black marble staircase toward the dark glistening pool, heading toward the shadows of the olive orchard.

It was hot in the grove—residual heat from the ground being stirred by pockets of cooler air as Nikki moved through the gnarled trees. The darkness felt thick. Ominous. And the scent of freshly watered ground was musky, dense.

Leaves rustled in gusts of wind. The flame of her torch sputtered. A small animal scrabbled through debris at her feet. Nikki jumped, heart jackhammering.

"Samira!" she called, throat dry as she held the flame up high. She moved deeper into the dark grove, farther away from the lights of the palace, the rows of knotted trunks taking ominous shape in her imagination. "Samira!"

Oh, please let me find you.

Something crackled leaves under the dark trees. Nikki froze, listening. The wind was picking up, shadows bobbing, leaves whispering and clicking as they rubbed together. It might have been a trick of her mind.

She inched forward, pulse racing. The torch sputtered in

sharp hot gusts, making shadows shimmy and lunge. Her heart beat faster—there *was* someone out here. She could feel it.

Abruptly a hand shot in front of her face, clamped down hard over her mouth. Nikki tried to scream, but the hand killed her sound. She dropped the torch, struggling and squirming to wrench the hands off her. But she was powerless against her assailant who dragged her kicking into the shadows.

"Make one sound—" a voice whispered in a guttural Arabic as a knife pressed up against her throat "—and the child will die."

Nikki froze, heart palpitating, sweat prickling over her body. *It wasn't Gelu!*

"You will be silent?"

She tried to nod.

Slowly the hand released her mouth. He turned her to face him, but his blade remained pressed tightly against her skin. Her assailant wore a black balaclava, black tunic and pants. He was not tall, but he was wiry, incredibly strong.

A second man materialized from the shadows. He was smaller, maybe just a boy, also dressed in black. He kicked sand over her burning torch.

"What do you want?" Her voice came out a hoarse whisper.

The larger man held what looked like a sophisticated PDA in front of Nikki. He pressed a key, and a small video feed flickered to life.

Samira.

Tied to a chair. Blade to her throat. Wrists bound by rope. Eyes terrified.

Nikki's hand flew to her mouth, almost to stop her own involuntary sound. Her gaze shot to the man.

"Now listen very carefully," he said. "Do as we say, or you will watch her throat being slit on camera, understand?"

"How…how do I know she's still alive?" Nikki shook with

fury. "What proof do I have that this was not recorded before you bastards killed her!" she hissed.

The man spoke into a cell phone, then held the screen for her to see as he gave her the phone. "Speak, and you will have your proof."

Nikki grasped the phone. "Samira! Can you hear me?"

On the small screen Samira's eyes flashed wide. She nodded.

The man yanked the phone away. "If you refuse to obey orders, the next time we show you this screen you will watch as she dies."

"What in hell do want from me?" she ground out through her clenched teeth.

The man clicked off the feed. "We have a man inside the Summer Palace—"

Gelu. He was *a part of this*. He'd *given these men access*.

"He knows there is a document in the Sheik's office."

Nikki's mind raced. The man referred to Zakir as sheik, not king. He had to be one of the insurgents unwilling to acknowledge his rule. Gelu was working for the insurgency.

"This document was delivered by two Sheik's Army generals today, in a metal tube. It's a map of key military installations. The Sheik has placed this tube in a drawer in his desk. It has this code on the tube."

A piece of paper was thrust into her hand.

"We know you have access to the Sheik's chambers at night. Get the contents of that tube while he sleeps. Bring it to us before sunrise. We will be waiting here, in the olive grove. Once this is done, we will release your orphan."

"That's insane!" she hissed. "He'll see me—"

"Which is why you will put this in his nightly carafe of wine." Nikki felt a capsule being pressed into her palm. "He will sleep soundly enough for you to enter his office unseen." He paused, allowing his words to sink in.

"Choose very carefully now. Whose life do you value more—Sheik Zakir Al Arif or your little pregnant orphan?"

She tried to swallow, tried to breathe, the man's words snaking ominously through her brain. "What…what's in the capsule?" she whispered.

"A narcotic to aid sleep."

Nikki felt sick. The smaller man handed the torch back to her, and he slid back into the night shadows.

"Before sunrise," the man reminded her.

"How…how can I trust that you will safely return Samira to me?"

"We want our country back more than we want to kill a little Mauritanian whore." He came closer, his voice lowering to a whisper that was almost lost in the rustle of the wind through the olive leaves. "And remember, we *do* have someone on the inside. He is in direct radio contact with us. If you breathe even one word of this to the Sheik, if he takes *any* countermeasure to save those installations on the map, we *will* know. The orphan will die at once. Make one mistake, and you'll live to regret it."

The man melted back into the night.

Bile rose to Nikki's throat. Shaking, she walked slowly back to the palace with her dead torch.

Zakir stood in his office after having summoned another cadre of men. The black blot in the center of his left eye seemed permanent now, expanding slowly. This additional tension didn't help. The candidates for marriage would be arriving tomorrow, and he'd made no headway with Nikki. Now this. He glanced at the gilt doors that hid a bank of LCD security screens.

There were security cameras installed in every palace room, all of them feeding continual footage into a digital database that was backed up hourly. His men had already gone through the footage from today, trying to find evidence of where Samira had gone.

The last digital image of Samira had been captured as she and the woman from the kitchen had left the kitchen entrance, making for the olive grove, baskets in hand. Just as the woman had testified.

Zakir did not have cameras in the orchards. Nor in the grounds beyond the patio and pools and private gardens. So he couldn't see what had transpired there. The next image was of the woman returning to the kitchen entrance with a full basket. Alone. She'd said Samira wanted to remain and walk in the orchard awhile.

Zakir drew back the gilt doors, exposing the bank of screens. He wanted to see that image again. But as he clicked on the monitors he was distracted by a live and grainy footage of Nikki emerging from the darkness near the pool, an unlit torch in her hand.

He zoomed in quickly.

Maybe it was the effect of the night light, but her face looked terribly white, eyes like black holes. Her posture was strange, too. Worried, he clicked off the screen, closed the doors and went to find her.

Zakir caught her making hurriedly for her chambers.

"Nikki!"

She spun around, eyes wide. Her face was sheened with perspiration.

"What is it? Where have you been?"

"I…I was out looking for Samira," she said, hand pressing to sternum.

"In the dark, in the olive orchard?"

She swallowed. "It was where she was last seen. I had to look one more time, Zakir. I am so worried about her."

He placed his palm on the side of her face, and Nikki felt herself involuntarily sag into his touch, desperate for relief, comfort. He gathered her into his arms, and held her tight. "You're trembling," he whispered as he stroked her hair.

"I…can't be alone tonight, Zakir," she lied, guilt twisting like a knife inside her. And even as she said the words, she knew she couldn't go through with it. She couldn't betray Zakir.

But she couldn't tell him, either. Not with Samira in his enemy's hands.

We do have someone on the inside. He is in direct radio contact with us. If you breathe even one word of this to the Sheik…we will know. The orphan will die at once.

The image of Samira tied to the chair, knife to her throat, surged into Nikki's mind. She closed her eyes against it, and Zakir bent down, kissed her lids.

"You taste of salt," he murmured. "Come to my chambers, Nikki. I will have a bath of rosewater prepared and fresh robes brought to you. I will hold you all night if you wish."

Her heart squeezed in pain. He cared for her. He respected her. He wanted to marry her.

And she was going to betray him.

Chapter 16

Before going to Zakir's chambers, Nikki went to check on the other orphans, buying herself a few minutes to try to figure things out. In the dark, she softly sang the song to them about the princess, her heart breaking as she thought of Samira in captivity somewhere.

When she heard the rhythm of the children's breathing change, she knew they were asleep, and she sat for a while in silence, watching the moon through the long arched windows.

If she told Zakir about Gelu—and what she'd been asked to do—he'd have no choice but to take immediate action against the traitor in his most intimate circle. Word would get out immediately. And they'd cut Samira's throat—she didn't doubt it. Nikki had seen enough terrible things happen on this continent to take those men very, very seriously.

Perhaps…if she just took that document, and got Samira back, she could then persuade Zakir to let them leave via chopper at once. And as soon as they were safely out of Al

Na'Jar—and Gelu's reach—she'd find a way to call him and tell him about Gelu.

She dug into the folds of her robe pocket. Fingering the capsule, she listened to the sound of the antique clock ticking.

It was now or never. And she had to move fast.

Nikki quietly edged open the bedside drawer where she'd seen Solomon stash the flashlight he'd been given to play with, then she tiptoed to the doctor's rooms that Zakir had allowed her to use. Quietly she clicked the door shut behind her. In the dark of the doctor's examining room, she studied the capsule under the flashlight.

It was opaque white, two halves slotted together—just like common cold medications she'd seen being sold throughout the northern desert. There was no pharmaceutical logo. Again, this was not unusual—certain black market medications were routinely marketed in Africa this way.

She turned the capsule over in the fingers. Nikki had absolutely no means of telling what powder was inside. The words of Samira's assailant slithered into her brain.

Whose life do you value more—Sheik Zakir Al Arif or your little pregnant orphan?

Why that choice of words—why the "life" of the Sheik? Could there be something other than a narcotic in this capsule?

She began to perspire all over again.

She glanced at the clock. He'd be waiting in his chambers for her. Wondering where she was.

She had to hurry, make a decision.

Nikki shut her eyes, inhaled deeply. Then she unlocked a smaller door that led into a medicine storage room. Shutting the door behind her, Nikki switched on the light and unlocked the medicine cabinet.

* * *

When Zakir came out of the bathroom, Nikki was sitting tensely on the edge of his large bed. She smiled at him, but light did not reach into her eyes. Zakir felt a pang of remorse at his inability to make things right for her, to make her happy.

She reached for his wine carafe, poured a glass and came up to him, letting her silk robe fall open as she handed him the drink.

Zakir went hot at the sight of her bare breasts, stomach, the small and seductive delta of hair at the apex of her thighs that hid her scar. He took the glass. "Are you sure you won't join me and have some wine, Nikki?"

She paled, shook her head.

Zakir frowned. "Nikki—" But she touched his lips with her fingers, quieting him.

"Drink your wine, Zakir," she whispered. "Don't take too long, because I want to make love to you." She was seducing him even in her sadness and worry.

He understood this—sex as a means of escape. It distracted one from dark thoughts. Being held by someone was comforting. "My men are still out there looking for her, Nikki," he said softly. "They have combed the olive groves and the orchards, and in the morning they will move farther afield into the village."

She nodded, reached for his hand, drawing him back toward the bed. Above them, through the glass dome, was a sliver of moon. It bathed the bed in a glow of silver. Allowing the silk robe to slip off her shoulders, she lay against the pillows, nude. Her eyes spoke to him, poignant, inviting him to drown in her.

His groin went rock hard.

Zakir took a large swallow of wine and plunked his glass down, an exhilarating warmth surging through his chest.

He opened her thighs and knelt between her legs. Lifting her hips to him, he thrust into her.

She gasped. Arched. And quickly spun over on top of him.

Her lovemaking was angry, desperate, fast. Hot. As if she was digging down deep for something she could not quite reach. Not at all like the tenuous exploration of yesterday. And Zakir climaxed so fast it shocked him.

She closed her eyes as she felt him come beneath her, and then, throwing her head back she shattered around him, sinking down onto him, warm, soft, her gold hair like silk against his naked skin.

A heavy tiredness descended over Zakir, like a weight stealing into his limbs. He felt strange, almost as though he was floating into darkness. The next instant his world went black.

Nikki waited until Zakir's breathing was heavy and regular. Then she felt his pulse to be sure he was okay, and she moved his head slightly to the side so he wouldn't choke. "I am so, so sorry, Zakir," she whispered, kissing him softly on the mouth, on his eyes, emotion tearing her soul apart. Then Nikki stood up, slipped into her robe, belted it tight and pressed her hand to her stomach.

Think of Samira.

If she could save Samira's life, she'd deal with the fall-out.

And she wouldn't blame him if Zakir made her pay. The best-case scenario was that they'd be gone from his country tomorrow.

Nikki dimmed the lights down low in case he woke up. She hesitated again at the corridor that led to his study, still torn. Running her hands over her hair, she glanced back at his naked sleeping form—all dark, masculine male. So powerful.

Yet she'd rendered him so vulnerable.

And in that instant she thought she could come to love him, and the notion cracked her right open. Hot tears filled her eyes. He'd offered her a life here, a marriage, a home for her children. All the things she'd ever wanted.

Who in hell are you kidding, Nikki? He's fallen for someone who doesn't exist. Your chance at happiness died seven years ago. You don't deserve him. You don't deserve happiness.

Nikki allowed the familiar self-loathing to course into her veins, steeling her focus, and she slipped down the corridor and carefully opened the door. She clicked it shut behind her, tiptoed into his study and flicked on a small desk light.

Zakir awoke in the dark hours before dawn, his head strangely thick. He could see nothing. He reached for Nikki, but the place she had lain in his bed was empty, the sheet cool.

"Nikki?" he whispered.

There was no answer from the darkness.

An edginess bit into Zakir. He clicked on the light.

She was gone.

He clicked it off again and lay back in the dark, a small hole forming in his soul. He should expect this. Nikki was going through a challenging night with Samira missing. Why should he anticipate she'd want to spend the whole night in his bed and wake with him in the morning?

And now that it was morning, what was he going to do? About her? About Samira? About those candidates being flown into Na'Jar? He couldn't push Nikki on the marriage issue—not while she was distraught over Samira's disappearance. And Tariq had not yet called with the results of the investigation. Conflict churned inside him.

Dawn was a peach strip on the horizon when Zakir heard his bedroom door open. He felt Nikki crawl back into his bed.

Zakir feigned sleep while she settled naked beside him. She smelled faintly of fire smoke, as if from a torch.

A cool curiosity rustled through him.

Perhaps she'd been in the private garden off her chambers, or perhaps she'd gone outside to look for Samira again.

When the sun flooded yellow and bright onto his bed and birds sang in the garden, he turned to her. She smiled sleepily, but her eyes betrayed her, and her features were tense.

"Did you sleep well?"

"Like a log."

"All night?" He watched her face.

"Yes, why?" Zakir saw a microflash of insecurity in her features, but she smiled at him again, seductively this time, and Zakir felt his loins stir in spite of his puzzlement, his stirring suspicion. Why was she seducing him now? Surely she'd rather be dashing out of bed at first light to resume her search for Samira?

The hole in his gut gnawed a little deeper.

He didn't like the strange sleep state he'd fallen into, either. His brain felt oddly fuzzy. Zakir suddenly lurched up from the bed, reached for his robe, belted it.

"I'll have breakfast sent to the garden for you, Nikki. But you must excuse me. I have some urgent work that must be attended to this morning. I need to liaise with my generals to organize ongoing security."

A glimmer of something akin to panic raced across her face, and she paled slightly.

Or was he imagining things? Was the light perhaps playing tricks with him even in sunshine now?

He went down the hall to his office, unable to cast off the cold sinking of foreboding hardening into him. Was it at all possible that he'd misjudged her? Could she have completely pulled the wool over his eyes with her orphans in order to gain his trust?

When he got there, he immediately found his documents missing from inside the metal tube he'd locked in his desk.

Zakir froze, rage surging through him like a tsunami.

His mind raced back over the night's events—the odd thickness in his brain, Nikki disappearing during the night, returning before dawn smelling of smoke. The fact she was not dashing out to hunt again for Samira…

No.

He could *not* accept it.

Zakir instantly went to the bank of monitors, flung open the doors, clicked the screens on. Quickly he rewound the footage from the hidden camera in his office. With a sheer sinking cold nausea, he saw an image of his desk light going on. The time on the bottom of the screen showed 2:00 a.m. Zakir's heart turned to granite as he watched Nikki opening his desk drawer, removing the papers from inside the metal tube. She replaced the tube in his drawer before clicking off the light.

White heat erupted in him.

He did not want to believe his own eyes. But the evidence was on that screen. He'd been such a fool!

She was a spy. She'd gone straight for the place where he'd stored the sensitive map. She'd duped him. Totally. And more.

Because once again he had fallen for a lie. And he'd fallen as hard as he possibly could have, even asking for her hand in marriage.

Just like all those years ago.

Blood pounded through his veins. Zakir fisted hands at his sides, and suddenly the vision in his left eye darkened to a solid black blot. It was quickly followed by a blurring in his right eye, as well.

He felt for the back of a chair, inhaled very deeply and blew air out slowly. Then angling his head so he could see through his peripheral vision of his right eye, Zakir clicked on the other screens, tracing Nikki's movements back through the night to the time Solomon first announced Samira's disappearance.

Sickened, he began to piece the images together. The cameras on the patio had caught Nikki going down the steps with a flashlight. She had a document in her hand. Zakir checked the time on the screen—2:40 a.m.

She must have met with someone in the olive grove and handed it over, because her hand was empty in the next image of her coming back up the stairs.

Zakir flicked to another camera that had caught her leaving the children's chambers with a flashlight, not long after midnight—just before she'd come to his bed. He watched as she headed to the doctor's examining room, glancing back over her shoulder as if leery of being followed.

Quickly he switched to camera footage from inside the doctor's examining room. It was dark, difficult to see what she was doing from the angle of her body, but she appeared to be examining something with the flashlight. Then she moved into the medicine storage room. Again her body obscured much of what she was doing, but Zakir could see her putting something in a small bottle. She placed it atop the cabinet, pushing it far back against the wall where no one would see it.

She then took some things from the cabinet and busied herself on the counter. Zakir zoomed in, the veins at his temple beginning to throb.

She seemed to be mixing a powder and putting it into a capsule. She then pocketed the capsule in her robe.

It hit him. *The wine.* How she'd held it out to him as she distracted him with the promise of sex, her naked body stealing the logic of caution from his mind.

And his heart turned dark and hard and cold.

Nikki had drugged him.

He clicked off the monitors, pressed the intercom on his desk. "Summon the two generals from the guest wing! Send them to my office at once!"

He walked to the arches that opened out over his garden, his dogs silent shadows beside him.

He hooked his hands behind his back, stared sightlessly out at his garden.

He could play the deception game, too.

Better than her.

More coldly than her.

And he held the advantage now. Because Nikki—if that was even her real name—didn't yet know that Zakir was aware she worked for his enemy. He'd keep it this way. And he'd use her to lead him back to the people who had murdered his father, his mother and Da'ud. The people who were trying to steal his country.

And once he found them, they would all pay—with their lives.

Including her.

Chapter 17

Before Zakir could order his two generals to mobilize protection for the new satellite installations they were interrupted by radio reports beginning to come in from across Al Na'Jar about bombings at the hidden military sites.

Zakir's jaw clenched.

Those installations were all marked on the map Nikki had stolen.

"The waves of sabotage will shut down military communications systems across most of the country!" barked one of his generals.

There was no shred of doubt in Zakir's mind now—the woman he'd invited into his home and his bed was a traitor. Enemy. Hatred sliced into his heart, and bitterness filled his mouth. He issued a rapid series of orders to his generals, who then clicked their boots with a slight bow of their heads and departed with staccato steps echoing down the halls.

Zakir pressed his intercom, called for one of his Gurkhas. While he waited for the man to arrive he poured water into a glass, quickly swallowing a handful of the pills Tariq had prescribed him to reduce blood pressure around the optic nerve.

When his Gurkha reported, Zakir instructed the guard to retrieve the small bottle Nikki had stashed atop the medicine cupboard in the doctor's rooms. He ordered him not to touch it with his fingers but to slip it into a paper bag. Zakir wanted to preserve the fingerprints on the glass.

While he waited for his Gurkha to return, Zakir placed his hands on the back of a chair, bent his head and closed his eyes, trying to gather himself, trying not to self-destruct with the fury of betrayal, or the pain he felt at allowing himself to fall—so damn hard—for another Juliet spy sent to seduce him in order to destroy the Al Arif dynasty.

How could you be such a fool!

What truly slayed him was the skill with which Nikki had manipulated his emotions, how she'd touched on the things so dear to him—his family, his love for the desert, his deep loyalty to his country. She'd deceived him with her apparent kindness and compassion, her knowledge of his people. And she'd apparently used innocent children to do it. Zakir had no doubt Samira's disappearance was now part of some elaborate scheme she'd cooked up once she found out via the Internet that he was going to marry one of those women to secure his rule.

Plus she'd coaxed him into revealing his Achilles' heel—his impending blindness.

Zakir swore softly.

She'd undoubtedly already passed this information to his enemies. He was going to face a challenge to his throne whether he caught her or not.

The Gurkha guard returned with the bottle in a paper packet. Zakir removed it using a piece of cloth. He held just the lid, lifting it to the light. Inside was one opaque white capsule.

"Take this pill and this bottle," Zakir said very quietly as he replaced the jar in the paper bag. "Have it flown via Black Hawk directly to the royal pathologist in Al Na'Jar. Tell him I want prints lifted from this glass, and I want to know what the powder inside this capsule is. And I want it before nightfall." He inhaled carefully. "If the pathologist needs laboratory access to identify the powder, get it, but make sure he is isolated. Because no one, understand, *no one* from the King's Council—not even my emissaries—can know about this."

As Zakir gave the orders, word came in over the radio of another blast. Yet another satellite installation had been sabotaged by insurgents and several more of his Sheik's Army troops had died in the explosion.

Zakir summoned two more Gurkhas and calmly, coolly ordered his men to have Nikki Hunt followed 24/7, but to never allow her to know that she was under scrutiny, and to give her free rein, even if she attempted to leave the palace grounds.

"Your goal is to learn who she makes contact with, then put tails on those people and follow them to additional contacts. I want to see if they'll lead us to the source of this insurgency." Zakir paused, the vision in his right eye now blurring again, as well. These episodes were coming back-to-back, and the darkness was not recovering in his left eye at all now. But he wasn't ready to go blind yet. He wanted to hold on to his vision long enough to look into Nikki's eyes when he sentenced her. To death.

"I want her every move recorded. Report back to me regularly."

Meanwhile, Zakir would mobilize the rest of his army for counterattack should Nikki lead him to an enemy base.

As soon as his men left his office, Zakir dialed Tariq's number. He paced, waiting for Tariq to pick up.

"Do you know what time it is here?" Tariq said, his voice thick with sleep.

"It's urgent, Tariq," he said quietly. "I have a possible lead to the insurgents. I need to know the status of the private investigation into Nikki Hunt."

"*She* is your lead?"

"Possibly."

"The same woman being vetted for betrothal? For queen of Al Na'Jar?"

Zakir pinched the bridge of his nose tightly. "Have they got anything on her yet?"

Tariq was silent for a moment. "I am sorry, brother."

Zakir cursed to himself. His brother had instantly deduced that once again Zakir had been led by his libido into a relationship with a female traitor. "There is nothing to be sorry about," he snapped. "The woman will lead us to our enemies, and that is what we want. But I need to know what our investigators have on her ASAP."

"I have not received a report yet—I'll call our investigators at once."

"Tell them that this woman's name is likely not Nikki Hunt. Her passport is probably false." Zakir hesitated, suddenly overwhelmed again by how deeply he'd fallen for her and how badly he'd wished she could be exactly who she'd claimed to be.

Several beats of silence hung between the continents. When Tariq spoke, his voice was quiet. "You're sure she's a fraud, *ya akhi?*"

"Certain of it."

"Does she know about your eyes?"

Zakir raked his hand over his hair. "Yes."

Another beat of silence.

"You cannot let her get out with this news, Zakir."

Instead of answering, Zakir leaned forward, clicked a key on his computer. "I am sending digital images of her face to your computer for biometrics cross-referencing. They were captured by our security cameras. I'll also be sending a scan of her fingerprints I'm having lifted from a glass bottle. I'd like you to pass these on to the investigators. Call me as soon as you know something."

Tariq studied the images his brother had just e-mailed to him. Frowning, he glanced up from his computer. It was dark outside, and snow fell soft and thick over the city, swirling in eddies beneath the yellow halos of streetlamps. Tariq got up from his desk, pulled down the blinds and returned to examine the stills Zakir had sent him. There was something so terribly familiar about the woman's face.

He swore he knew her from somewhere.

Nikki was distraught. She'd gone down into the olive grove during the dark hours of dawn while Zakir was drugged, and she'd handed the document over. But the men had not returned Samira. Instead, they'd informed Nikki they'd bring her the next night, if the map checked out.

And today something was going down. A sense of urgency had taken over the palace. Soldiers moved with focus. Choppers thudded over the fortress fetching and carrying important-looking people who moved in and out of Zakir's office all day. The king himself had remained sequestered there.

Then Nikki heard news of bombings being whispered by kitchen staff. And more attacks throughout the country. No one was looking for Samira, either, which disturbed Nikki.

Stressed beyond words, she paced up and down the length of her room.

If Zakir found out what she'd done, she would certainly face trial.

Death.

She needed to get Samira back tonight, and she had to find a way to get the hell out of here, maybe using all this action as a distraction. Nikki left her room and quickly made for the children's chambers. There she packed a few bags, getting the younger children ready. She told them to remain in the chambers and to be prepared to move at a moment's notice. And she instructed them to remain silent, to tell no one—not one single soul—that they were ready to evacuate the palace.

"Solomon," she whispered, crouching down to eye level, "I am putting you in charge, okay?"

He nodded gravely. "What about Samira?"

Nikki bit her lip, her heart squeezing at the liquid emotion gleaming in young Solomon's big round eyes. These children has seen so much darkness in their life that they absorbed bad news with stoic acceptance. "She's coming back tonight, Solomon. I promise," she whispered very quietly in French. "Keep this to yourself, okay?"

He nodded, one lone tear rolling like a jewel down his dark cheek. Nikki bit back her own emotion. "And Solomon, if something happens to me, go to the staff in the kitchen and get someone to show you how to leave the palace. Try to find your way back to the Rahm Hills. The Berbers will take care of you."

"What could happen to you, Miss Nikki?"

"*Rien,* Solomon. Nothing. But just in case the king gets angry with us—"

"He can be an angry man?"

"I think he can be a very angry man."

Especially when he finds out what I have done to him.

At dinnertime there was still no sign of Zakir. Unable to

eat, Nikki declined the food the palace staff brought to her. And when the sun sank behind the red and brown peaks and a hot velvet darkness swallowed the land, Nikki made sure no one was following her, and she went down into the olive garden.

A different man stepped out of the shadows. Bigger. Rougher.

Her grabbed her, doused her torch and yanked her back into the trees.

"Where is Samira?" she hissed with mounting panic as she saw no sign of her.

"You did not follow orders," the man growled in broken Arabic.

"I did! *Where is she?*" Frantically, Nikki peered into the dark shapes between the twisted trunks and branches of the ancient olives. But there was nothing. "You bastard!" she swore, lunging for the knife sheathed at his hips, grabbing the hilt. She yanked it free, but the man's hand clamped like a vise over her wrist. He twisted her around, wrenching her hand up high behind her back, and he shoved her cheek hard into the gnarled bark of an olive tree.

Nikki's heart thudded as she felt the tip of his knife press against her carotid artery. Somewhere in the back of her mind she registered that it was a hunting knife, not a jambiya or kukri.

"You lie," he whispered, his breath hot against her ear. And it hit her that he was not a native Arabic speaker, but she could not place the accent. French or Italian, maybe. He twisted her arm higher, and she gasped in pain. He dug the blade against her skin.

"What," she said hoarsely, "makes you think I didn't follow your orders?"

His mouth came even closer. She could smell mint and a

particular tobacco, black, bitter. A hint of aftershave. This man wore gloves.

"Because," he whispered, mint-tobacco breath feathering hot over her lips, *"the Sheik is still alive."*

She froze, heart palpitating. *"That's* what you wanted from me? The pill—it was supposed to kill him?"

The man removed something from his pocket. She noted he was wearing jeans, a Western shirt. He keyed his PDA, held it in front of her eye, the other side of her face still squished against rough bark. The screen on his PDA flickered to a gray glow. Then an image came up.

Samira.

A hood over her head, jambiya at her throat. The man holding the blade wore a balaclava.

Nikki's assailant gave a command into the device, and the hood was ripped from Samira's head. Nikki choked at the sight of her orphan's terrified eyes, the dried blood on her mouth, one eye swollen shut. "Wait!" she whispered. "Please…please don't do anything. I…I used another drug on the king, a barbiturate. I thought it would be easier to medicate him with it because I was familiar with the dosage and could be certain how long he'd stay under. With the capsule you gave me…I…I was unsure."

Leaves rustled.

"You still have the capsule?"

"Yes," she said hoarsely. "I have it. It's in a jar on top of the cabinet in the physician's examining room."

"You will use it, then. Tonight. The poison will take between eight to twelve hours to work. If Sheik Zakir Al Arif is not dead by tomorrow evening—" he thrust the PDA image of Samira in front of Nikki's nose "—she dies instead."

"Then you will have won nothing," Nikki rasped as he continued to press her face hard against the tree.

"And neither will you." He spun her around suddenly,

moonlight glinting in his dark eyes that showed through the balaclava slit. "Will you do this?"

Nikki stared directly into his eyes. The skin around them was pale. He was Caucasian. "What guarantee do I have that you will honor *your* word?"

"She's not dead yet, is she?"

"That's because she still holds currency for you," spat Nikki. "She's still got leverage."

He hooked his gloved knuckle under her chin, forcing her face up. He brought his lips so close they almost skimmed hers. "If you do this," he whispered, "she *will* go free. And if you do it well, no one will know that it was you who assassinated the Sheik. We don't want you or the girl. All we want is for the Al Arif dynasty to die. For too long they have ruled this desert. It is now our time."

He let her go, and like a black ghost, he slipped back into the trees.

Nikki began to shake violently. She braced her palm against the tree, bent over and threw up. Then she crouched down, searching for her doused torch amongst the sharp, dry leaves. The air in the grove was hot, the leaves rustling as the breeze stirred. But as Nikki located her torch, she heard a crunch of twigs. She stilled. Then she heard it again, another footfall.

"Who...who's there?" she called nervously, drawing her veil back over her face.

She thought she heard another sound, as if the footsteps were retreating.

Nikki waited in the shadows for a long while. She had no idea what to do. And nowhere to turn.

When Nikki reentered the palace, all was disturbingly silent.

She peeked in at the kids. They'd had dinner and were either reading or climbing into bed, their bags still packed and under their beds. Solomon came up to her door. "What happened, Miss Nikki? You have scrapes on the side of your face."

She forced a smile. "*De rien. Je suis bien.* Thank you for holding the fort, Solomon."

"Where is Samira?"

"She…she's on her way. I just have a few things to do first."

"Are we to remain all packed and ready to leave?"

"Yes. And thank you, Solomon. You have no idea how much of a help you are." She kissed the top of his head and made her way to the physician's examining room. Closing the door quietly behind her, she leaned against the wall, head back, eyes closed. Cold nausea swirled in her stomach.

She'd been pushed right up to the edge. This was far worse than she could ever have imagined. Both Zakir's and Samira's lives were in danger. And she was in the middle. She had no doubt that Gelu was working with these men. He was probably planning for her to take the blame if the king died.

Now she *had* to tell Zakir that his enemies were planning to assassinate him. And she had to do it very, very carefully, because if Gelu found out, it would be death for Samira. Nikki would have to somehow convince Zakir to play along and feign ignorance at least until Samira was safe.

But would he do it? Especially after she told him that she'd spied on him, drugged him, stolen a critical document?

Even if he did, she doubted he could ever forgive her. He'd have her tried for treason.

Telling Zakir she'd spied on him might just help save Samira, but it was going to come at a huge personal cost. She'd lose her own life. But what other choice did she have?

Because there was no way in hell she'd ever even think of giving him the poison.

Nikki exhaled shakily, her body wet with perspiration.

She had to do it. Now.

She had to make the sacrifice—lose everything, including her precious children—to save his life and hopefully Samira's.

She had to take the capsule of poison to him and confess it all.

Nikki leaned up on tiptoes and felt with her fingertips along the top of the cabinet for the pill bottle she'd stashed there. For a terrifying moment she thought it was gone, then her fingers brushed against the bottle. She had to fetch a stool to reach it. She must've pushed it farther back than she'd realized.

Nikki retrieved the capsule and slid it into her pocket.

She exited the room and stepped into the marble corridor.

"Nikki!"

She jerked stiff, spun around. In shock she saw Zakir marching down the passage tightly flanked by Gelu and Hasan. He held on to his dog as he strode, tall, unfaltering. Impeccably dressed, scimitar gleaming.

Nikki's heart leaped against her chest.

Up until now, Zakir had done without his bodyguards in the private living quarters of the palace. Something had changed. She wiped damp palms against her skirt. "Still…still no sign of Samira?" she asked.

"My men are searching everywhere and everyone," he said curtly. "I am sure you saw the helicopter activity, all the troops arriving and going?"

That was more than a search and rescue mission for Samira.

She nodded.

"They're going through the outlying village now. House by house. And—" he paused, eyes narrowing "—where were *you* going?"

From behind Zakir, Gelu's eyes caught hers in warning,

his hand moving surreptitiously to the hilt of his kukri knife. Fear balled into Nikki's throat.

"I...I was just coming to look for you. I...needed to talk to you...about something."

"Good," said Zakir, taking her arm brusquely. "You can talk while you dine with me."

Something had changed in the king. He had to have noticed the scratches and blood on her face, her state of disarray, yet he said nothing.

And Nikki was suddenly terrified of him.

Gelu and Hasan slotted the bolt across the inside of the dining hall door and took up positions in front of it.

Panic flared in Nikki's eyes as she saw this, and she turned to Zakir. "I...was hoping we could dine in private," she said, her voice thick.

Zakir pulled out a chair. "Things have changed. Take a seat." She did, nervous, her gaze flicking to Gelu and Hasan.

It hardened Zakir's heart. He saw her fear as just another sign of her guilt. Flipping out his napkin, he poured wine into two crystal goblets. "You will join me tonight, Nikki. Partake of my fine cellar collection."

"That...doesn't sound like a request, Zakir."

"It's not."

Blood drained from her face. "I...don't understand."

Zakir smiled harshly at her, hating her for her beauty, for breaking his heart, for killing his family, for making him taste the intoxicating pain of need.

But he'd regained the upper hand.

His other Gurkhas had seen her in the grove tonight, and they'd followed the man she'd met with. That man had led them straight to a large military-style bunker dug into a cliff wall. The Sheik's Army was now busy surrounding it. Without Nikki's betrayal, Zakir would never have found it.

This was exhilarating news. It was, however, tainted by the fact Zakir had then watched Nikki from the cameras in his office as she returned to the medicine room. He'd watched as she retrieved her capsule from the jar atop the cabinet and slipped it into her skirt pocket. And she had it with her now.

Thanks to his pathologist, Zakir now knew what the powder was—a highly toxic cyanide compound.

She wasn't just a spy.

She was an assassin.

Chapter 18

Nikki stared at the burgundy liquid Zakir was forcing on her, fear rearing like a horse in her heart.

He didn't blink. Not a muscle in his body moved. "I must concede, Nikki, that you ply your craft exceedingly well."

"Excuse me?"

He leaned forward suddenly. "Did your people compile a psychological profile of me, assess my weaknesses? Then send in someone specifically selected to target my vulnerabilities? Is that why you came up with the idea of playing a mission nurse? And where did you get the children for your ruse? Steal them from some orphanage?"

Panic licked through Nikki. She shot a glance at the door. The Gurkhas blocked access, their hands on their knives.

Zakir waited for her gaze to meet his again. When it did, Nikki's mouth went bone-dry. His face had turned to dark thunder, eyes crackling with aggression and hatred. There was no sign of the man she'd been falling in love with, the man who'd asked her to spend the rest of her life with him.

"What is your name?" he said very quietly in Arabic. "Your *real* name."

Blood leached from her face. It was over. This was it. Her brain raced—she'd take whatever punishment he chose to mete out, but she *had* to find a way to make him help Samira. And she could not do that with Gelu standing there listening to every word.

"Zakir, I—"

"Damn you!" He slammed his fist on the table, making silver cutlery jump. "You are the worst kind of traitor to a man."

"Zakir, please—" Nikki reached out, covering his bunched fist with her hand "—this is not what you think."

He glowered at her, vibrating under her touch. And she caught a sudden glisten of emotion in his fierce eyes. Her heart crumpled, and a lump wedged into her throat.

"I was falling for you," he whispered darkly. "In the way that I had fallen for only one other woman. I knew you had something in your past that you wanted to hide, but I suspected it was some personal pain over a lost child, a broken relationship. But I did *not* believe you to be a cold-hearted, calculating enemy!" He paused, watching her. Dark silence vibrated through the room. "I watched you with those orphans in the Rahm Hills. I listened to you sing to them. I talked to the Berbers about the shepherd you'd saved. I came to believe your lies. Instead, I find you are a spy."

Tears burned into her eyes. "Zakir…that is not true."

Zakir slowly got to his feet, jaw tight, neck muscles cording, eyes narrowing in aggression. He came to Nikki's side of the table, clamped his fingers in a cuff around her wrist. Nikki's heart skittered.

Drawing her forcibly up from her chair, Zakir's eyes tunneled into hers. Nikki couldn't breathe with fear. She felt dizzy.

Abruptly he yanked her body hard against his, thrust his fingers into the hair at the nape of her neck and gripped so tight it made her eyes water. He bent his head, pressed his lips on hers, forcing her mouth open, his tongue entering angrily. Tears rolled down Nikki's face as he pulled her even closer, cupping her buttocks. Then he caught her lip between her teeth and applied pressure. She froze, tasting blood, sensing danger. Slowly he released her lip and whispered over her mouth, "Is this how they trained you to do it? To go for the groin? To work my libido? To kiss and screw someone you plan to kill?"

She swallowed, tried to pull back. But he increased his grip. Her pulse jackhammered. Sweat prickled over her brow.

"And what kind of woman puts children into danger, using them as props for an espionage game?"

Nikki tried to open her mouth to speak, but he covered it with his own, silencing her while he moved his hand around the side of her hip. She felt it slipping between the folds of her robe and into her pocket. *The pill—he knew it was in there.*

Her breath caught, and her heart stopped.

Slowly he extracted the capsule from her pocket. He brought it up to her face, held it right in front of her nose.

Nikki went ice-cold.

"What's this?" he whispered.

"Zakir—

"Tell me!"

She tried to swallow. "That…that's cold medication. I… was feeling ill."

"You have a cold?"

"Yes."

"I see." He held the capsule over the goblet of red wine he'd set in front of her. Zakir split the two halves of the capsule apart, spilling a dusting of fine white powder into the burgundy liquid. Nikki gazed in horror as the poison dissolved into the dark wine.

He forked his index and middle fingers around the stem of the crystal goblet, lifted it. He held the poisoned drink out to her. "Drink, then. It'll make your cold better."

"I…I told you…I…I can't…don't drink Zakir. I…"

"I will believe *nothing* you say until you drink that medicine!" He shoved the glass into her hand. "Take it!"

She did, her hand beginning to shake. "Zakir, please, listen to me. I am not a spy—"

"You—" he said very quietly, darkly "—were captured on camera stealing a document from my office. And you say you are not a spy?"

Her eyes flicked to Gelu. "I…I never wanted to deceive you, Zakir. You have *got* to believe that."

"Your deception—" his voice was dangerously quiet "—cost the lives of my men. You cost me millions in equipment. Your deception has destroyed military communications in my country. Now drink that wine."

The poison inside will take between eight to twelve hours to work.

And then where would that leave Samira?

"Zakir, please listen to me. I never intended to hurt you. I am deeply sorry about what happened. More sorry than you can ever imagine. But I am *not* a spy. I'm not your enemy. I came into Al Na'Jar by mistake, seeking only safe passage for my orphans. You were kind. You helped us, and…and you made me believe I could fall in love with you," she whispered, emotion pooling hot in her eyes. "Believe me, I wanted nothing more than to accept your proposal, Zakir," she whispered. "To stay here with my children. To be your wife. But…I couldn't." Her voice caught. "Because you are right. I am hiding something. But it's personal. Not political—"

"What is it?" he snapped.

"I…I'm not Nikki Hunt."

A muscle began to quiver at the base of his jaw, and his body crackled with dark energy. Hatred filled his eyes. "Who are you? And," he said quietly between clenched teeth, "if you lie to me now, my wrath will know no bounds."

Nikki inhaled shakily.

If she could get Zakir to believe her real background, maybe she could buy back a measure of trust. Maybe she could still find a way to save Samira.

But she could feel Gelu's eyes on her.

"Before I tell you who I am, I ask for just one thing, Zakir. No matter what you decide to do with me, please do not punish my children. Please promise that you will give them safe passage to the mission on Tenerife."

"I make no promises to you," he said coolly. "But I also don't harm innocent children."

Nikki nodded, moistened her lips. "My real name is Alexis Etherington, and I'm not a nurse," she said very quietly. "I'm a doctor, an ophthalmic surgeon, and the reason I won't drink this wine, Zakir—" she glanced down at the glass still in her right hand "—is because seven years ago alcohol nearly killed me. At the time I wished it had." She wiped her upper lip with the base of her thumb. Zakir saw she was trembling.

"I'd experienced a terrible loss, and I didn't know how to go on. I was using any substance I could find to self-medicate, to numb the unbearable agony that ate at me."

"What agony?"

She inhaled deeply. "My husband hired someone to kill me. The man tried to run me off the road on Christmas Eve seven years ago. He didn't know that my twins, Hailey and Chase, were sleeping in the back of my car. He hit my vehicle on an icy bridge. I went into a spin. It was snowing heavily, and I went right through the railing and plunged onto the highway below, where we were instantly hit by a semi."

She fell silent, a haunted look entering her beautiful eyes. "My daughter, Hailey, died on impact. Chase took a little while longer. He died in hospital. I…I was trapped. I couldn't get to him, to help him."

Surprise streaked through Zakir.

This angle he did not expect. But he cautioned himself against showing sympathy. This woman had come to him with a highly toxic poison in her pocket—a uniquely prepared cyanide compound designed to kill him. Yet he couldn't help wanting to hear the rest of the story that she was now spinning. And she was doing it with such apparent honesty in her clear, sad eyes that he desperately, achingly, wanted to hear it. And to believe it. And he detested himself for this need.

"Carry on," he said coolly. "Why would your husband try to kill you?"

"Because he's a sick man. He's been diagnosed as a narcissistic sociopath and he keeps it well hidden. He is also very smart, very ambitious, and he can be exceedingly charming. He dupes people, uses them for his own gain, and then spits them out when he's done. And he was done with me. He was having an affair. I found out and was going to file for a divorce, and he knew he'd lose access to my inheritance and trust fund if I was successful. He'd also lose custody of the children if I got my way. So he tried to have me eliminated instead."

"How do you know this?"

"I…can't prove it, but I suspected that I was being watched, followed by someone in a black SUV. It almost ran me off the road once before."

He raised an eyebrow, but Zakir said nothing.

"Then, after a Christmas party, the same black SUV was waiting outside my friend's house. I'd gone for a drink after work, but my sitter was sick, so I took the kids with me. The vehicle followed me from the party and the driver managed to send me into a spin on the snow- and ice-covered bridge."

"Why," said Zakir slowly, "would your husband want to kill his own kids?"

"He *didn't*. That was a mistake. The driver of the SUV didn't know my children were in the car that night. And when Sam learned what had happened he lost it. He was beyond furious, and he tried everything in his considerable power to blame me for 'killing' his children."

Zakir thought of her scars. The Caesarean. Twins. It was possible. He shook himself. She was smart. It could all be lies. She could be sucking him in again.

"While I was still recovering in hospital, Sam leaked information to the press, claiming that I had been driving drunk, that I was an alcoholic and drug addict and that I'd cancelled surgeries in the past because of it. My blood tests confirmed that there was a small amount of alcohol in my system because I'd had one glass of wine at the Christmas party. The cops dropped it, but a journalist ran with the story anyway. I had my privileges at the hospital suspended, pending investigation. Zakir," she said, her voice thin, "I didn't even have the will or energy to fight him, or the hospital, or the cops or my friends who weren't sure whose side to take. I was injured myself. But more than anything I was devastated beyond grief over the loss of my two babies." Tears filled her eyes as she spoke.

Zakir's heart torqued. Yet again, he chided himself to be cautious.

"I drowned in bottle after bottle of alcohol. I lost my medical license and my practice. But Sam wasn't content to just let me drown like a pathetic lush. When the cops dropped their criminal investigation, he slapped me with a civil suit of his own, claiming I'd killed his children. I was a pariah. I was a shaking, stinking mess. I got to a point where I didn't care whether I lived or died anymore."

She swayed slightly, glancing at the chair. "Stand," he commanded. "Tell me who your husband is. Why should he hold so much power? Why would the press be so interested in his and your lives?"

She lifted her eyes to his and his heart spasmed. Zakir swallowed, at war inside in his own body.

"My husband is Sam Etherington. He's a senator being groomed for a run at his party leadership. He's after the top office in the U.S."

Something in Zakir stilled. "And you say your name is Alexis Etherington?"

She nodded. "Dr. Alexis Etherington, an ophthalmic surgeon from Washington, D.C."

He digested the enormity of this revelation. Could this be why she'd blanched at the mention of Tariq? His brother's interests lay in a similar field. They came from the same city.

"How did you end up in Africa?" he asked.

"I was saved by a television commercial for Mercy Missions. It showed two children, a boy and a girl, about the same age as Hailey and Chase. I…I was suddenly riveted by the image, their big eyes. The innocence. And then I heard the ad saying that Mercy Missions was a foreign organization that sets up bases in troubled countries where children are forgotten. They send in priests, nuns, teachers and nurses." Her eyes brimmed with emotion, and Nikki fell silent for several beats, trying to compose herself. "This ad was looking for volunteer nurses. Those two children spoke to my heart, Zakir. They told me I still had a role to play in this world. And somehow it gave meaning to this terrible spiral I had descended into. I took it as a sign that I was not supposed to kill myself. I was supposed to get *this* message. I was destined to help save lost children.

Which is what I've been doing in Mauritania for the past six years."

"You still haven't explained your new name, your passport, your papers."

"My husband and I had a lot of parties over the years, attended by a lot of government employees. One of them was an ex-CIA operative who once drunkenly told me if I ever wanted to buy a fake ID, he knew how. I laughed it off back then. But I remembered, and I looked him up. He organized the forgeries for me, including fake nursing papers. I paid him a small fortune. As soon as I had them, I left the country."

The story rang so true. The emotion in her eyes, in her face appeared so real. He longed to believe her...

"Remember, Nikki," he said softly. "I will verify this. If I find one word of what you say now to be false—"

"It's the truth, Zakir." She sounded completely resigned, as if all energy in her body had been spent. And again compassion curled into the fire raging inside him.

He shut it down irritably. "Finish your story."

She looked directly into his eyes, just as she had on the first day he'd met her. "I am not a weak woman, Zakir. I am not easily beaten. But the loss of my twins and Sam's attack... I crumpled in the worst possible way. It was humiliating, and it fills me with self-loathing, but there is nothing I can do to change that. All I can do now is save my orphans." Her eyes flicked nervously to Gelu.

"Samira especially," she said. "I need to save Samira."

Zakir frowned inwardly. She'd been glancing at Gelu like that all the time they'd been in here. But not at Hasan.

"What do you mean, save Samira? Do you know where she is?" Out of the corner of his good eye, Zakir saw Gelu shift. And he sensed Nikki stiffen in response. There was some kind of hidden communication happening between the two.

It made him even more suspicious. Was it possible they

could be working together. This woman and his most trusted guard?

And there was still the problem of the poison in the glass in her hand.

She began to speak again, but he held his hand up abruptly, silencing her. "It's an interesting story, Nikki. Or Alexis. Or whoever you are—"

"It's the truth."

"Then prove it," he snapped. "Drink that wine."

Panic flared in her eyes.

And his heart went stone cold. There was no doubt in Zakir's mind from the look in her face that she knew exactly what the capsule contained.

"Zakir—"

He grabbed the goblet. "You say it's cold medication?"

She glanced at Gelu, then nodded, face sheet-white.

"Then I will drink it!" In one swift movement he raised the crystal rim to his lips and swallowed the entire contents of the glass. He braced as warmth fired across his chest, and he slapped the glass down on the table.

Her mouth fell open in sheer horror. For a nanosecond, she was unable to speak.

Then she suddenly lunged forward, grabbed his arm, terror racing across her face. "Zakir! We need to get you to a hospital! Fast!"

He glowered at her fingers digging into his arm, then he lifted his gaze to meet hers. "Why?"

"There was poison in that glass! It'll kill you within twelve hours."

"So you came to assassinate me," he said darkly. "Just as I suspected."

"No! Zakir, please, just get to a hospital—"

"You are despicable, you know that," he whispered. "The worst kind of liar." He shook off her arm and marched toward the gilt double doors, clicking his fingers for his dogs to follow. "Open the doors!" he commanded.

His Gurkhas slid back the bolt.

"Zakir!" She lurched after him, grabbing for his arm. "Please, God, *listen* to me! We have to get you to a hospital now!"

He swiveled around. "Why should I listen to someone who came to assassinate me?"

"I would *never* have given that poison to you. They tried to make me do it. That's why they took Samira."

"*Who* tried to make you?"

She shot a terrified glance at Gelu. "If I tell you they'll kill her, Zakir."

"And how would these people know that you told me?"

"I…I don't know."

He shook her off angrily. "Take her away from me!" he barked to his guards. "Lock her in her chambers. Both of you stand guard outside, and do not budge an inch until I send relief, understood?"

She fought against the guards as they grabbed her roughly by the arms. Tears sheened down her face as they dragged her away. "Please, Zakir…please just get to a hospital. You need medical attention or you'll *die*."

Unease whispered through Zakir, and inside he faltered. But he turned his back on her and marched down the corridor, making straight for his office, dogs in tow.

Immediately, he pressed the button on his intercom. "Send in my generals."

The men entered his office with a click of their heels and bow of their heads. "Take some armed men up to Nikki Hunt's chambers. She's being held prisoner there. Two of my Gurkhas are guarding her outside the door—Gelu and Hasan. I want you to take Gelu by surprise, shackle him and put him in the dungeon. Hold him for questioning."

Surprise showed in their eyes.

"It's a simple precaution."

Anything was possible. And Zakir had not liked the subtle interaction he'd witnessed between Gelu and Nikki.

"Go!" he ordered his generals. "Now!" *Before Gelu has time to leave his post and possibly contact someone on the outside—or free Nikki.* Zakir was leaving no base uncovered.

The doors swung shut, and Zakir groped for his chair, his left eye still completely blind, a blur whirling in his right. He sensed he didn't have long before his world went dark.

Forever.

Chapter 19

Gelu believed he'd won. He wasn't sure how it had all happened, but it had played in his favor. The king had swallowed the poison. And Nikki Hunt was being held for treason. Hasan would bear witness to that.

All that remained for Gelu was to kill Nikki Hunt so she couldn't point a finger at him. He'd pretend she was trying to escape. He'd do it as soon as he saw the opportunity. Then he'd call his handler in Al Na'Jar, tell him the news and collect the bonus he'd been promised upon completion.

Gelu saw the Sheik's Army soldier approaching too late. Part of his mind thought it was his relief from guard duty, but there was something ominous in the man's stride, the way he was holding his semiautomatic rifle. Then Gelu saw soldiers coming from the other side. And it slowly dawned on him—they were coming to arrest him.

But before Gelu could draw his blade, the soldiers had him at gunpoint.

* * *

The shutters in Nikki's room had been locked and the light filtering in from outside was faint. But she knew from the clock on the wall that over thirty-six hours had passed since Zakir had swallowed the poison.

If Zakir had died, maybe there was a chance that Samira had been spared. But she'd probably never know.

Nikki paced the length of her dim chambers again as she'd dazedly been doing since she'd been locked up, her mind beginning to play tricks on her. She'd replayed the final scene in the dining hall over and over again. Zakir had taken her by such surprise that she hadn't even had time to register what he was doing, let alone react and stop him. She still didn't understand what game he'd been playing.

Nikki swung around, retraced her steps again, her breathing shallow, her body drenched in sweat.

She'd come so damn close to tasting hope again.

Instead, she'd failed. Herself. Her orphans. Zakir.

She didn't care if they executed her now—she had nothing more to live for.

Nikki stilled at the sound of choppers coming in to land. Men were yelling, screaming. Sporadic gunfire peppered the air. Fighting had started. The country was turning to chaos.

This was her fault.

Whichever way the cards had fallen after she'd been dragged from the dining hall, she was responsible for this. She'd aided the insurgents by giving them that document, and she'd brought the poison that had killed Zakir into the palace.

Who would have thought when she'd marched up that palace boulevard that she'd end up here? Responsible for the downfall of this kingdom, when all she'd wanted was safe passage to the sea.

Suddenly, things went strangely quiet outside.

The dead silence grew eerie. Hot.

Nikki stopped pacing again. It was as if the battle were over. Exhausted, she slumped onto the side of the bed and allowed her body to slide down onto the marble floor. She put her face in her hands.

Darkness spiraled into her brain as she drifted in and out of consciousness. And then mercifully, she slid into oblivion, her world going black.

Tariq left his computer for a moment to light the fire in his study. As he listened to the blizzard wind whistling outside, he again thought about the face captured on Zakir's security footage. And it hit him so hard and sudden that it stole his breath.

Was it possible?

Quickly he seated himself at his desk and fired up the Internet, running a search of newspaper stories from six to seven years ago.

It *was* her—Dr. Alexis Etherington. He was sure of it.

By God...how could this be? He sat back in his chair, ran his hand over his hair. Maybe he was making a mistake, seeing something that wasn't there. He needed to check, be certain, before he called Zakir. He reached for the phone, dialed the man heading up their private investigation.

"That file I asked you to work on, cross-reference the information you already have on Nikki Hunt with the name Dr. Alexis Etherington, an ophthalmic surgeon and the wife of Senator Sam Etherington. She disappeared from the D.C. area about six years ago. She and the senator lost twins in a car accident a year before her disappearance. There was a police investigation, allegations of drunk driving. The security footage I forwarded you shows a woman who looks identical to Dr. Etherington, but I can't be sure. Is it possible to run a biometrics comparison scan of the security footage against an old passport or an ID image or maybe one of the media photographs?"

"It is," said the man. "I'll have an answer for you as soon as we secure an image of Dr. Etherington."

Tariq paused. "Look, I know I don't need to reiterate this, but we're heading into potential diplomatic conflict here if this is the senator's wife. I need this information to remain strictly private."

"Understood."

Tariq hung up, leaned back in his leather chair, thinking of the newspaper and television coverage seven years ago, and how stunned he'd been to hear what had happened to Dr. Etherington.

Such a tragic story. Such a beautiful and talented doctor, someone he'd admired, respected and whose work had helped him identify the genetic markers of Naveed's Hereditary Optic Neuropathy in his own brother. Tariq had been astounded by the way she'd fallen from grace, then vanished—only to turn up in the court of Al Na'Jar? This was remarkable.

Tariq's phone rang, and he grabbed it.

"Dr. Al Arif, the security images are a one hundred percent biometrics match to old media photographs of Dr. Alexis Etherington. The fingerprints from the medicine jar that your brother forwarded to us are also a match. The person captured on the security footage *is* Dr. Etherington. It appears she assumed the identity of Nicola Ann Hunt, a deceased infant born in the D.C. area."

Tariq signed off, quickly punched in the number for Zakir's encrypted satellite phone. His fiancée peeked around the door as Tariq listened to the phone ringing in the Sahara.

She smiled at him, her dark hair falling seductively over her face. "When are you coming to bed, Tariq?" she said softly, her brown eyes sparkling. "It's getting cold in there."

His heart warmed at the sight of Julie's face and the caress of her voice. "Give me a minute," he said.

But there was no answer from Zakir's private phone.

"The compound is surrounded, your Highness. We're ready to strike."

"Do it." Zakir's heart felt cold, black, empty as he clutched the military radio, unable to see again for a moment. He closed his eyes. "I want as many alive as possible for interrogation purposes." He hesitated, hearing Nikki's words.

They kidnapped Samira. They said they'd kill her if I didn't take the document.

"There might be a pregnant girl being held hostage in the compound." He cursed himself for *still* wanting to believe Nikki's words. "If she's in there I want her unharmed." Zakir would not be able to live with himself if it were true and his raid caused Samira's death. He signed off the radio as a Gurkha handed him his satellite phone.

"Someone's been repeatedly trying to get through."

"Yes!" he barked in Arabic.

Zakir tensed when he heard Tariq's voice, and his fist tightened around the phone as he listened to his brother relate the tragic story that had gripped the media seven years ago—the exact same story Nikki had told him before he swallowed the fake pill. Hope flared deep and hot in his gut.

"You're *sure?*" he whispered.

"We have a fingerprint and biometrics match. She's the woman I met at that conference, Zakir."

His heart raced. He closed his eyes again. It was easier than straining to see.

"She's the one who led me to test you for the markers all those years ago. It is because of Dr. Etherington that we are prepared for your loss of vision."

Zakir thought of Nikki's appearance in his country, how

she'd walked right into his life. As if they were ordained to meet.

He thought of the way she'd watched his eyes so intently, and he recalled how she'd stared at the sight of Tariq's photo in the dining hall and the subsequent mention of his name. If she remembered what Tariq had approached her about at that conference all those years ago, she'd have put two and two together after she'd seen Zakir stumble. Nikki had known exactly what was happening to him almost from the get-go.

"Go on," he said quietly to his brother.

And Tariq related how the terrible tragedy had played out in the media, how the doctor's husband had sued her for allegedly driving drunk and killing his kids.

It all meshed. Every word.

He inhaled deeply, recalling her scars, the way her body had moved naked against his, and in his mind he saw every detail of her face, the look in her eyes. And his own eyes filled with hot emotion.

"She secured the fake identity just before leaving the States, Zakir. Our people are pursuing that angle."

She really had come to the Sahara to save children, because she'd been unable to save her own.

"Get them to rush on it," he said quickly. "Tell them to contact Mercy Missions again. Get the exact dates she applied, joined them. Everything. Every little piece of that puzzle! I want it!"

He hung up, heart thudding, and he radioed his general out in the field.

"Any numbers on captives or injured yet?"

"We lost only five men—"

Zakir cut to the chase. "The pregnant girl?"

"We have her. She's safe."

Emotion, relief surged through him. "Bring her to the Summer Palace at once!"

Zakir signed off and yelled for his Gurkha. "I want a full medical team flown here stat. There's already an obstetrician on the way, but I want a psychologist as well, someone with experience in critical incident stress debriefing. Set up the medical rooms in preparation. And get me our top interrogator from Al Na'Jar. I want him here within the next ninety minutes. Understand? I need him to question one of my guards."

"Yes, sir, at once your Highness."

He ran his hands over his hair, his skin beginning to tingle with exhilaration.

She was telling the truth.

He reminded himself to proceed with caution. Samira would be delicately questioned, Gelu more forcibly. *Every* detail must be verified before he could think of going to her.

The door to Nikki's room opened, and a shaft of bright yellow light cut into the room.

She blinked up from the floor. Zakir's silhouette loomed into the frame of light. He stood silent, his dogs unmoving at his side, the jewels on his scimitar hilt glimmering.

For a moment Nikki thought she must be dreaming.

He stepped into the room using his dogs to guide him, as if he couldn't see. He wore his black shades.

Quickly, she tried to get up to her feet, but a sharp wave of dizziness and nausea forced her to sit on the bed for a moment.

He quieted her with a wave of his hand, and he turned to face the door.

Another figure, slight, stepped into the shaft of light.

Samira!

Nikki couldn't breathe. Or move. Or even think as she saw the two people who meant the most in her world standing side by side.

Both alive?

"Miss Nikki?" Samira said softly, coming up to her. Emotion surged into Nikki's chest, and tears seared into her eyes. She got up, took hold of Samira's thin shoulders, then dropping to her knees in front of the teen she urgently felt for broken bones, cuts, bruises, for signs of baby movement. "Did…did they touch you, Samira?" she whispered, voice thick.

"Not in that way, Miss Nikki."

"You…you're okay…." She choked on the words as exhaustion and emotion welled out of her, tears rolling hot down her face.

"I missed you, Miss Nikki," Samira whispered, clamping her arms tightly around Nikki's neck. "But I knew you would fix things. I knew you would send the king's men to get me."

Nikki shot a glance at Zakir. "You…you found her," she whispered, still in shock, not quite believing anything.

Zakir nodded. But she could tell from the way he was holding his head that behind his glasses he wasn't seeing much. If at all. Her heart wrenched.

"I've brought in a team of doctors for Samira," Zakir said quietly in Arabic. "One is a psychologist. And the obstetrician is now waiting outside to take Samira in for a proper checkup to see if the baby is all right."

She sniffed, wiping her face with her sleeve. "Go, Samira. I'll come see you again as soon as the doctor is done. So will Solomon and the others."

"Thank you, Miss Nikki."

Nikki covered her mouth with a shaking hand, tears spilling down her face again as she watched the girl leave the room. Then she turned to Zakir. "Oh, *thank you,*" she whispered.

He reached out, took her arm. "It's my pleasure, too, to see her safe."

"You can't see, Zakir, can you?"

"Not much. The vision is gone in the left eye. It will be soon now."

She led Zakir to the bed and sat beside him. "I am so sorry."

"I am prepared for this part."

"What…what happened with the poison?"

"After you were caught on the security camera hiding the bottle, Nikki, I had the capsule replaced with a placebo while I sent the contents to be analyzed in Al Na'Jar."

Just as she'd replaced the poison by using a known sedative the first time.

"I needed to know if you were trying to kill me."

"I would never have given it to you, Zakir. I replaced the contents of the first capsule they gave me with a sedative, because I couldn't be sure what was in it. But when I gave them the document, they kept Samira and tried to force me do it properly the second time around. I was coming to confess. I was going to hand the capsule over to you. Except you brought Gelu. He was—"

"I know, Nikki," he said quietly. "I became suspicious of him in the dining hall, the way you were catching his eyes. At first I thought you might be collaborating. I had him immediately imprisoned for questioning. It turns out he's been freelancing for my enemy on the King's Council, Fakhir Nasab. I also have him in custody now. Nasab paid Gelu a great deal of money to spy on me and later to attempt an assassination."

"Nasab is with the insurgency?"

"It's not clear yet. My interrogators believe Nasab might be using the insurgency to create unrest for another reason. He might be working for someone else, possibly even for someone outside the country. We have a lot of work to do still. The danger is not over."

"Zakir, in the orchard, the man who gave me the capsule and the orders, he was foreign. Caucasian, I think. He had an accent that might have been European, maybe French."

Zakir nodded. "We have him. My men followed him from the orchard after he met with you. He led us to an insurgent cell, a base camp carved into a sandstone cliff. They were holding Samira there."

Emotion balled into her throat again. For a moment she couldn't speak. She touched his hand, his smooth dark skin, her heart swelling and aching with love for this fierce and gentle man. So strong, yet so vulnerable in his impending blindness.

"Zakir," she whispered, "can you forgive me for—"

He touched his fingertips over her lips. "I know you didn't come here to hurt me, Nikki. My heart was right. You are a healer, not a killer. Tariq helped confirm this. He remembered who you were, and he passed the information to our private investigators in the States. They confirmed it with biometrics and fingerprint matches."

She inhaled shakily, Sam snaking back into her thoughts. With it came the cool, dank fear, the memories. "I am not that person anymore, Zakir."

"Nor am I the same person you saw written up in the tabloids, Nikki." He paused. "Sometimes we need to go through a crucible of trials to become the people we are really destined to be."

Silently, she reached up, removed his glasses. Nikki touched the sides of his eyes, and her heart sank. His right pupil was showing barely any reaction at all. He was almost completely blind.

He touched her face in return, his strong fingers so gentle, and as he felt the wetness on her cheeks, emotion began to glisten in his own eyes. "I am thankful that I can see you one last time, before the darkness is permanent. I'd like to think you were destined to come to me, Nikki," he whispered. "I think we could be good together. I believe we *belong* together."

She crumpled against his strong body. And he stroked her hair. "Tell me about your twins," he whispered. "About Hailey and Chase. Tell me everything."

And she did. It was the first time Nikki had been able to speak openly about it in this way, without feeling judged, hated, and it was profoundly cathartic.

Zakir gathered her tightly into his arms. He held and comforted her like she'd needed to be comforted all those years ago after the tragic deaths of her toddlers. Like she'd needed to be loved by the husband who'd betrayed her.

"What about the senator?" she whispered as her emotions settled. "Does…does he know I am here?"

"Nikki—" for she'd never be anything else to him "—Senator Etherington will never know. Your identity will remain a secret between us and our private security company. Omair has special contacts who can create you a brand-new identity. One that will withstand exhaustive international scrutiny. But we can keep the name Nikki." He caressed her face. "I would like this, because you *are* Nikki to me. And the surname they choose is irrelevant because—if you say yes—when you become my queen you will adopt the Al Arif name and legacy as your own. *That* is the name that will matter."

Tears were streaming down her face again. Zakir could feel the hot wetness. He could feel her shaking. But he could see very little in this light. He leaned down, kissing the tears away, tasting the salt of her emotion, remembering every little detail of her oasis eyes, her features, the memory of her face glowing like a candle—a beacon of light and hope in the darkness that would now become a part of his life.

"How can this be done, Zakir? How can you just give me an identity that will withstand such scrutiny?"

He inhaled, thinking no more secrets. What he knew about Omair, she, too, would know. "Omair sometimes contracts to a private military organization based on Sao Diogo, an island off the west coast of Africa. This company occasionally subcontracts to the CIA or the Pentagon. Omair tells us very little about his work, Nikki, but I do know his people can organize this. I have already spoken to him about it. Nikki Hunt will cease to exist. She will have fled the mission in Mauritania and vanished, presumed perished in the Sahara."

"What…about my orphans?"

"We will make them ours, Nikki."

"All seven?"

He laughed. "Eight if we count the new baby that will be born in the Summer Palace. They, too, can bear the Al Arif name. It will mean a lot to me." He smiled, feeling warm, feeling a sense of family, feeling like a true patriarch. All things he'd missed and begun to crave upon his return to the desert. Things he'd begun to crave when he'd met Nikki.

He sensed her shift in energy, her joy, and Zakir reached up to touch her mouth. He felt her smile. His heart soared. It gave him such pleasure to make her happy, to give hope back. To protect her.

"What about Mercy Missions, Zakir? You mentioned that you told the Tenerife base that I was here—"

"We'll work it out. We can say any number of things, for example, that we lost contact with you again when you returned to the Rahm Hills."

"And your enemies on the King's Council—what if they've already dug up something on my past?"

"Those enemies are all now in custody, Nikki. They will stand trial at once, and anything they know will go with them to their graves. We still do not yet know who was pulling their strings, but if we do this quickly—if we change your identity and we marry very soon—you *will* be safe." He cupped her face. "Will you accept my proposal and become my queen of Al Na'Jar? Will you rule by my side and help guide me when I stray?"

"Zakir, what if some journalist tries to trace my background and finds I am this person with no history?"

"Omair's contacts are the real deal, Nikki. They'll plant a false past for you. And they—and I—will make sure that Sam Etherington can't touch you."

By leaking to the press that he had tried to kill his wife.

He lifted her face to his. "Please, Nikki, be my queen. Rule by my side. And in return I promise to protect you and keep you and our children safe."

"Yes," she whispered, not believing this was possible. Not fully able to comprehend that her ridiculous childhood fairy-tale dreams had come true—she'd found her prince. She'd found family. After all she'd been through.

"I love, you, Zakir," she whispered as she leaned up to kiss him. "More than you will ever know."

Zakir took her into the private garden off his chambers, where she bathed in rosewater, the sun warm on her naked skin. And they made love again, so tenderly and so poignantly, and Nikki felt as if she had come home. Into the arms of her sheik. Where he would keep her safe. And loved. Always.

And she would guide him through his darkness in return.

* * * * *

Kay Young returned to woozy consciousness to find that she was lying on a soft sofa beneath a heap of quilts near a cheerfully burning fire. When she tried to move, however, everything hurt, and she groaned.

At once she heard a sound, then a stranger with a hard, harsh face was squatting beside her. "Shh," he said softly. "You're safe here. I promise."

"I have to go," she said weakly, struggling against pain. "He'll find me. He can't find me."

"Easy, lady," he said quietly. "You're hurt. No one's going to find you here."

"He will," she said desperately, terror clutching at her insides. "He always finds me!"

"Easy," he said again. "There's a blizzard outside. No one's getting here tonight, not even the doctor. I know, because I tried."

"Doctor? I don't need a doctor! I've got to get away."

"There's nowhere to go tonight," he said levelly. "And if I thought you could stand, I'd take you to a window and show you."

But even as she tried once more to pull away the quilts, she remembered something else: this man had been gentle when he'd found her beside the road, even when she had kicked and clawed. He hadn't hurt her.

Terror receded just a bit. She looked at him and detected signs of true concern there.

The terror eased another notch and she let her head sag on the pillow. "He always finds me," she whispered.

"Not here. Not tonight. That much I can guarantee."

Will Kay's mysterious rescuer protect her
from her worst fears?
Find out in HER HERO IN HIDING by New York Times
bestselling author Rachel Lee.
Available June 2010, only from
Silhouette® Romantic Suspense.